W9-BVU-325

FICTION
Mye

Myers, Anna.

The grave robber's
secret

DISCARD

DUE DATE   MCN   04/11   16.99

TWEEN FICTION M

The
GRAVE ROBBER'S
SECRET

ALSO BY ANNA MYERS

Red-Dirt Jessie
Rosie's Tiger
Graveyard Girl
Spotting the Leopard
The Keeping Room
Fire in the Hills
Ethan Between Us
Captain's Command
When the Bough Breaks
Stolen by the Sea
Tulsa Burning
Flying Blind
Hoggee
Assassin
Confessions from the Principal's Chair
Wart
Spy!
Time of the Witches

The GRAVE ROBBER'S SECRET

ANNA MYERS

WALKER & COMPANY

New York

First published in the United States of America in February 2011
by Walker Publishing Company, Inc., a division of Bloomsbury Publishing, Inc.
www.bloomsburykids.com

For information about permission to reproduce selections from this book, write to
Permissions, Walker BFYR, 175 Fifth Avenue, New York, New York 10010

Library of Congress Cataloging-in-Publication Data
Myers, Anna.
The grave robber's secret / Anna Myers.
p.   cm.
Summary: In Philadelphia in the 1800s, twelve-year-old Robbie is forced
to help his father rob graves, then when he suspects his dad of murder,
Robbie makes a life-changing decision.
ISBN 978-0-8027-2183-9
[1. Grave robbing—Fiction.   2. Murder—Fiction.   3. Philadelphia (Pa.)—
History—19th century—Fiction.]   I. Title.
PZ7.M9814Gq 2011   [Fic]—dc22   2010018097

Book design by Nicole Gastonguay
Typeset by Westchester Book Composition
Printed in the U.S.A. by Quad/Graphics, Pennsylvania
2 4 6 8 10 9 7 5 3 1

For two lifelong friends, Charlene Richardson Sasser and Darlene Fast Crofford. I am so glad we shared our childhoods and life's journey

Philippians 1:3
I thank my God upon every remembrance of you.

The
GRAVE ROBBER'S
SECRET

CHAPTER ONE

There was no moon when Robby first went to the grave-yard at night. On the broken front stoop of his home, he waited, wrapping his arms around his thin body as best he could, partly for warmth against the chill of the early spring night and partly in an effort to slow the beat of his heart. He searched the sky for a star, but not even that small light could be seen—a dark night for a dark task. His father, Roger Hare, came around the corner of the house with a wheelbarrow that Robby had never seen. Without a word, he picked up his shovel, put it over his shoulder, and moved from the shadow to walk behind his father. Robby expected no conversation between them on this journey, but Da wanted to boast about acquiring the cart.

"Picked up this little beauty back of a house over on Society Hill." Da waved his hand in a gesture of dismissal. "They got plenty of money to buy carts. Yes sirree, Bob!"

Robby made no reply, and the streets of Philadelphia were quiet, so that the words of a town crier drifted from the lane behind the house. "Three o'clock and all's well!" Robby's stomach tightened. He made his free hand into a fist, but he relaxed his fingers because, of course, he could not hit his father. He wished he knew how to relax his stomach.

After the town crier, Robby heard nothing except the sound of a barking dog and the cart wheels on the cobblestones. The walk was a short one, and too soon he could see the rock wall that enclosed the graves. His feet felt heavy to lift, but he struggled to follow the bulky figure moving in front of him to the stone archway entrance with its black iron gate. For one joyful moment, Robby thought the gate might be locked, but he was wrong.

Da waved Robby forward. "Open it, boy. Hurry!"

Breathing hard, Robby moved around his father and pushed against the gate. The metal felt cold, but it was not as heavy as it looked. He opened it wide enough for his father to move the wheelbarrow through. Inside the cemetery a big willow tree grew just to the right of where Robby stood behind the open gate. In the darkness he could not see if new leaves were appearing on the thin branches yet, but he was almost certain he saw movement among them. What creature hid there?

"Close it now," his father said, and he traveled on down the path, not waiting for Robby, who made himself catch up.

The darkness felt thick, like a huge black-velvet blanket draped over the path and over the headstones, only the white ones visible. No stone marked the fresh grave, but Robby knew he could find it. He had been there earlier and had traced the route in his mind until he had memorized it. Soon the path would divide at a crossroads where a white angel statue marked a grave, and as he turned his head to look to the left for the angel, he stepped into a hole. His shovel fell from his shoulder and he waved his arms in an attempt to keep his balance. Before he could stop himself, he cried out in surprise. It was not a truly loud sound, but it cut through the still night. Da would not overlook the blunder.

Roger Hare put down the handles of the wheelbarrow, which held another shovel, a metal crowbar, a rope, and a long sack Robby's mother had sewed from white material. He leaned over Robby and thumped his massive thumb hard against Robby's head. Then he grabbed the boy's arm and yanked. "Up with you and mind your step, you little imp," he muttered, giving Robby a final rough jerk. "I brung you out here to give me a hand, I did, not to go stumbling about and shouting at the top of your lungs." He turned and tromped on, leaving Robby to push the cart.

When the path forked, Da stopped. "Which way? Quick now!" Robby wanted to lie, to lead his father in circles through the graves until the sun rose and made their ghoulish mission impossible. There could be no grave robbing in daylight with carriages going up and down the busy street just beyond the rock wall. He gritted his teeth. Not taking his father to the fresh grave would never work. He did not think Da would go so far as to actually kill him, but Robby had suffered a beating at his father's hands before.

"That way," Robby said, pointing toward the angel, and after only a few steps, they saw the mound of newly turned earth.

"Don't just stand about gaping," said his father. "Get to the other side and start digging."

Robby did as he was told, pushing his foot on the shovel with all his might. The wooden shovels did not slide through the earth as well as metal spades would have, but Robby knew the wooden ones had been selected because they were quieter. He stared only at the earth he moved, careful not to look at his father. Maybe he could run away. He had planned to do so last night, but in the light of day, his courage waned. Roger Hare was a huge man with powerful fists that could come down hard on Robby. Still, Robby was fairly certain he could at least outrun him. The problem was he had no place to go. Da was certain to find him, and besides, there was his mother to consider.

An owl hooted from a nearby tree. Maybe it was the owl that had been in the willow. The sound came again, and Robby thought the bird called out a warning about disturbing the grave. Just then he heard the thud he had dreaded.

"There we go! I've hit the coffin," Roger Hare said with pleasure. "Fetch me bar from the cart."

Robby scrambled out of the hole, took the crowbar from the cart, and handed it to Da, who stuck the end of the bar under the lid of the coffin and pushed with all the strength in his hulking body. Robby moved his lips in silent prayer. "Let the lid hold, please God, just let it hold," he pleaded, but he soon heard a cracking sound. He looked down to see his father lift the top half of the coffin lid, but blessedly he could not see the face in the dark hole. "Get the rope and hop down here, boy. You can do the tying."

Robby's stomach turned. "Please, Da, no," he whispered. "Don't make me." But he knew he would have to do it. Still, he couldn't force himself to move until his father had hauled himself from the hole.

"Down with you, boy," Da said, "else I'll shove you, I will."

He stretched out his arm toward Robby, who jumped before he could be pushed. The top part of the coffin was open now, but all Robby could see was a white cover. "Get the cover off her," said Da. With a shaking hand, Robby touched the soft white blanket and pulled it away from the face and chest. His father dropped the looped end of the rope down. "Slide it over the shoulders, boy," he said.

Despite the cool night, sweat poured down Robby's face. He put out a hand to grasp the loop, but his trembling made it impossible to catch hold until he used two hands. He knelt down on the part of the coffin lid that was still intact. Now he had to look at her. He had seen the body earlier in the day, forced as he was to attend the funeral and to walk with the mourners to the cemetery. "You're not afraid of the dead," Robby told himself. Hadn't he helped his mother prepare the body of his little sister for burial? He swallowed back the bile that rose in his throat. No, he was not afraid of dead bodies, but he was desperately afraid of grave robbing.

Da had come home early from the pub last night with the grave robbing idea, bursting into the kitchen, where Robby and his mother had been finishing washing the supper dishes. "There's considerable money to be made," he had announced, "and we ain't going to break no law. Nobody owns a dead body, and that's a fact. We can't be charged with stealing if we be careful not to take the clothes nor the shroud nor nothing buried with the body."

"Still, it's dangerous," Robby's mother had said, turning from her dishpan. "Wasn't a fellow beaten almost to death just a few weeks ago when he was caught?"

"What's it to me if he was?" Da pulled a chair near to the

big black kitchen stove. "I'm a deal smarter than most men, I am. I'm not likely to be caught, now am I?"

Robby's father had laid out his scheme then. A girl had died just that morning. "Just a slip of a thing, ten years old, they say. Still, her body will bring as much as one full growed," he had said. "And it won't be heavy to lift."

"Then why must you take Robby?" Ma had pleaded.

"Hush, woman. I am taking the boy. In fact, I've just had me a brilliant notion. Our boy will be attending the funeral tomorrow, joining the mourners at the grave site. No one will notice the likes of him. He can put the location in his head, so as to lead me. It won't do to have us wandering around the cemetery looking for the spot. The longer the job takes the more the chance we have to be caught."

That night Robby tossed about on his pallet before the kitchen fire. Deep down he knew he would never run away, but he liked to pretend he might. Before he left for the funeral, he could take what bread was in the kitchen, wrap it in a cloth, and carry it beneath his shirt. The resolution made it possible for him to sleep. The next day, though, he had gone to the funeral, slipping into a seat at the rear of the church. Her name was Ruth Caldwell, and he saw that her parents were wild with grief. When the mourners filed past the casket, he had hesitated to go, but at the last minute had changed his mind. He wanted to look on the girl's face. He had stood for a few seconds, looking down, and had been consumed with guilt. "I'm sorry, Ruth, so awful sorry," he whispered, and then he had moved on.

Only this morning his mother had tried again to prevent his father from including Robby in his new moneymaking scheme. Breakfast had long since been over, but Da still sat at the table smoking his pipe. "Come now, Roger," his mother had pleaded, "he's but a child."

His father had turned to where Robby stood in the doorway, having just come in to pump water for his mother to heat for washing bed linens. "How old are you, boy?" he demanded.

"Twelve," Robby murmured, and he moved to the kitchen pump.

"Huh? Speak up, boy!"

"Twelve years old," he all but shouted, and he wanted to add, my name is Robby. He hated how his father almost always called him "boy."

"Twelve!" thundered Da. "It's long past time you did something to bring in money."

"But he does," protested his mother. "I couldn't manage here, couldn't keep this boardinghouse without Robby's help. Please, Roger, if you be determined to do such gruesome work, don't put our Robby into the mix. God knows what might happen if you're caught."

"Gruesome, is it?" Da pounded the table. "I say that me selling bodies to the surgeons will save lives, that it will! Besides, the money is good, a better wage than ever I've earned at some ordinary job."

Robby caught his mother's eye. He knew that like himself she was trying to remember the last time Roger Hare had brought home money from any job. He liked better to sit at the table, smoke his pipe, and criticize whatever his wife or son might be doing.

"It's all right," Robby whispered to his mother when he passed her with the water bucket. "Don't fret about me."

He did not want his mother to argue more with Da, who might suddenly go into a rage and slap her hard.

He had tried not to think about Ruth as he followed the mourners to the cemetery, staying always at the back of the crowd. He had wanted only to memorize the path, but now standing in the girl's grave the guilt came back, and his loathing for what they were doing made him sicker than he had ever felt before.

Da leaned over from above him. "What is it, boy?" he said in a voice that sounded like a growl. "Get the rope around her shoulders now! We ain't got all night here!"

Robby slipped the loop over Ruth's head. His hand brushed her face, and her skin felt cold. "Just get it done," he told himself. "Get it done." He had to lift her head and shoulders slightly in order to slide the rope under. Her dress was white, and Robby remembered that little pink flowers were embroidered in the material. He touched one on a sleeve, then arranged the loop over her shoulders. "I'm finished," he said to his father, and he started to climb up.

"No, boy, stay put. You'll be needed to give her a lift. I can't tug too hard. Those bloody surgeons won't buy a body already pulled apart, you know."

Robby drew in a sharp breath. He did not want to touch Ruth again, but he had to do what his father ordered. Besides, he could not bear to see the body torn apart. Da pulled gently on the rope, and Ruth began to rise. "Yes, sir," said his father. "Yes sirree, Bob, we're raising her out of the grave, ain't we, boy? You and me, we're resurrection men. That's what we are." His voice sounded proud.

Ruth's lifeless form proved easy to pull, and Robby had

to lift only once just as the lower part of the body came out of the coffin. "Come on up, boy," his father told him then. "I can get her easy now."

When he had climbed out, Robby picked up a shovel to begin filling the grave with dirt, but his father stopped him. "Not yet." Da began to slip the white dress over the body. "We got to put this dress back. It's a shame, likely bring us some nice coins, but we can't take no chance of being arrested for thieving. Not on your life."

Robby did not watch his father remove the dress or put Ruth's body into the white bag his mother had made. He did see the dress after it fell from his father's hands back into the open casket. He put the lid back on, and he began to shovel then, shovel with all his might, lifting and tossing spadeful after spadeful; he was almost finished by the time his father had arranged the body in the cart. When the grave looked as it had before the theft, they moved silently to the path, Da pushing the wheelbarrow with the shovels tucked in on either side of the bag. Robby carried the crowbar over his shoulder.

Da led the way. Near the cemetery gate, he lowered the cart. "I'll just pop out and make sure there ain't no nosy people wandering about," he said.

Robby's heart beat fast. He was not certain what he wanted. Did he hope no one would catch them? If they were discovered, there would be trouble. Likely his father would fight his way free and run, leaving Robby there to take all the punishment. Still, wouldn't that be better than being successful? If they escaped detection, there would be other midnight robberies.

Again Robby saw a movement in the willow tree. This time

he moved closer and parted the limbs. It was a woman! When he could make out her face, Robby recognized her. She put her arm up as if to ward off a blow. "Leave me be," she muttered.

"It's me, Robby," he whispered. "Don't you know me, Jane? I'd not hurt you, not ever."

Just then he saw that his father was back inside the cemetery. He waved Robby forward, and picking up the cart handles he began to push. "What in tarnation was you doing mucking about that tree?" Da asked over his shoulder. "We ain't out here on a lark."

Robby's mind raced to think of a response, but to his relief Da did not seem to expect an answer. It would not do for Da to know about the woman everyone called Daft Jane hiding in the tree. Robby's mother sometimes took in the poor creature to give her a meal and helped her clean up a bit, but never when Da was home. Robby couldn't trust his father not to hurt Jane if he suspected she had seen them take the body.

The street was deserted, no one in sight except for a man and a woman who leaned against one another in a doorway. They were too interested in each other to look at a boy and his father with a wheelbarrow.

Pennsylvania Hospital was a huge brick building on Pine Street. It stretched across a full block between Eighth Street and Ninth Street. Robby had seen the big building many times, but he had never dreamed he would be going inside to sell a body in the dead of night. Da steered the cart to a small door at the back of the east wing. A faint glow showed through a nearby window, proving that somewhere a lantern burned. "This here is the school part," he said, and he set down the cart. "They say you got to bang hard, hard enough to wake the dead." He laughed at his choice of words and began to pound.

Finally, the door opened. "Can I help you?" The man inside was neither young nor old. He had a thin face and kind eyes. His hair stood up on his head, his clothing in disarray. Robby thought he must have been asleep. He carried a lighted candle.

"It's me what can help you, sir," said Roger Hare. "That is if you be a doctor."

"My name is Dr. Bell."

"This here is your lucky day, Dr. Bell," said Roger, and he smiled broadly. "We've got a body for you. Fresh too, just buried today."

The doctor stepped out of the doorway, went to the cart, leaned over, and opened the bag. "Oh," he said, "this is a child."

"Her name is Ruth," Robby said. His father gave him a little shove.

"Keep your mouth shut, boy," he said. "Her name don't matter now."

"I imagine it matters to her parents," said the doctor.

"They won't never know she ain't still in the grave. Why all this talk?" said Da. "You take young ones, don't you?" He folded his arms across his chest. "Young'ns slice up same as grown ones, don't they? I want full pay."

The doctor shot him an angry look. "You're a tenderhearted fellow, aren't you?" He turned to Robby. "Hold this candle for me," he said, and he gathered the body bag into his arms. "Well, follow me," he said over his shoulder.

Robby hung back. "I'll wait here, Da," he said, but Roger reached out to grab his arm.

"You'll come along with us," he ordered.

The three walked down a dark hall, their steps sounding loud on the wooden floor. A strong medicine-like smell filled Robby's nose. The doctor led them into a large windowless room, where two candles burned. Dr. Bell placed the bag on a long table. He turned to take the candle Robby held and began to light six gas lamps that were fastened to the walls. Robby could see the loft now on one wall. Stairs led up to it and seats were arranged there in three rows at graduated heights. The doctor noticed Robby looking at the loft. "Our students sit there," he explained. "So they see what is done here on the floor."

He came back to the table again and started to slip the bag away from the body. Robby had hoped to be out of the room without seeing Ruth again, and he turned his head quickly away. On the wall just beyond the table was a drawing of the human body. Each organ and bone had a name written beside it. Robby stepped away from the table to study the diagram, but from the corner of his eye he could still see his father and the doctor.

"You've got to check the goods, I reckon," said Roger Hare, "but let me remind you that I ain't been paid. That body's still mine, it is, until I get the money, yes sirree, Bob." He held out his hand, and Dr. Bell reached onto a nearby shelf for a metal box from which he took bills. He counted them and then placed them in Da's hand.

"Now be gone with you," he said, but Da shook his head.

"I'll be troubling you to give me back me bag," he said. "My missus just sewed it up for me, she did, and there will be need of it again."

Robby still gazed at the drawing. He'd had no idea there were so many things inside a body. "Is this really how it looks inside . . . of a person, I mean?" He had not meant to speak, and he looked down, self-conscious.

Dr. Bell turned to lay his hand briefly on Robby's arm. "Yes. Fascinating, isn't it?" he said, and he smiled. He pointed to the heart. "A heart is about the size of a fist, and it pumps blood to every part of the body."

"And if the heart stops, a person dies, right?"

The doctor nodded. "The blood caries the oxygen we need to live." He smiled at Robby. "What's your name, son?"

"Robby—" He was about to add the last name, but his father interrupted.

"We ain't here for no conversation." Da held out his hand. "Me bag?"

Without a word Dr. Bell finished removing the bag, covered the body with a sheet, and handed the bag to Roger. "I'll let you out," he said, and they followed him back to the door.

When Da had stepped from the building, Robby turned quickly to the doctor. "Is Ruth's heart small because her hands are small?"

"Yes, the heart grows at about the same rate the hand does." He smiled at Robby. "Maybe you would like to come back sometime and look again at the chart or other things here."

"Oh, thank you." The invitation pleased him, but he wanted to forget the place and the reason he had been inside. Da reached back, jerked Robby forward, and pushed him back the way they had come.

"That one's high and mighty," he said when the door was closed. "He's a butcher, that's what he is! He ain't got no right to be looking down on the likes of us. At least we don't go about carving up little girls."

Robby hoped his father would say nothing more, and Da was blessedly quiet as they walked the dark streets toward home. They had gone only a few steps when a cold rain began to fall. Robby felt glad. The rain chilled him, but he felt it might also cleanse him. He held his hands out to get every drop.

It continued to rain until they turned onto the street where their house with the broken stoop stood in the middle of a long row of houses, all two stories and made of red brick. In the dark and at first glance, the Hare house did not look so different from the others. But in the daylight an observer would notice that besides the broken board on the stoop, shutters hung loose from two of the front windows. The wooden door frame wanted painting too. Robby wondered if he could fix the shutters himself. Da would never get around to them.

They cut through the alley between the houses to go to the back door. A light shone through the kitchen window, and Robby knew his mother had worried all the time they had been gone. She looked up from mending when the door opened. "God be praised. You're safe," she said when she saw Robby.

"Safe?" said Da. "Of course we be safe. No man in these parts wants to tangle with Roger Hare." He held up the crowbar he had taken from the wheelbarrow he left near the door. "Any man who tried to get in me way would have found hisself wearing me trusty bar here through his head. I'm starved, woman. I'll just go change me wet clothes while you get me some vittles."

Robby had gone immediately to position himself before the stove. His mother took a bowl from the cupboard and came to stand beside him. "Are you hungry, son?" She took the cover from a big pot that sat on the back of the stove and filled a bowl. "I've got some stew with a bit of mutton in it."

He shook his head no, but he did not speak. She set the bowl on the table and laid the palm of her hand against his cheek. "It was terrible hard for you, and I'm dreadful sorry for such a thing to fall to you."

Robby swallowed back the sob that wanted to escape from inside. If he cried, his mother would feel even sorrier. Besides, tears would help nothing. He jammed his hands into his pockets. "I'll not do it again, Ma," he said. "I'll run away before I do it again."

His mother's eyes darted toward the hall from which Da's steps could be heard. She laid a finger against her lips. "Ssshh! He mustn't hear you."

"I won't, though," Robby said quietly. "I'll run away if I have to." The look in his mother's eyes made him immediately sorry for his words.

"Oh no, Robby, please don't say such a thing."

Roger Hare came into the kitchen then from his bedchamber, and Robby went through the swinging door into the parlor and on into the hall, where he sat on the stairs. He stretched his legs across the third step. Using his arms for a pillow, he rested against the step above him. Maybe tomorrow someone would come to take a room, or even better, maybe two people would come. Surely if the rooms were taken, his father would not go out at night to steal bodies. Robby closed his eyes.

His mother woke him with a gentle shake. "He's gone to bed now," she said softly. "I've laid your pallet out. You'll feel better tomorrow," she said, and she bent to kiss his cheek.

CHAPTER TWO

He did not feel better the next day. Da slept late, but Ma was up as usual making breakfast. "Miss Stone needs breakfast," she told Robby when he pulled his quilt over his face.

Old Miss Stone was their only boarder. She had seemed increasingly frail over the last few weeks, and most of the time Robby carried her food up to her. He loved to be in her room because of her books, filling a big bookshelf to overflowing.

Miss Stone, who had been a teacher in her younger days, had read from her books to Robby, and she had used them to teach him to read. He could still remember the thrill he had felt when he sat beside her with the red primer in his lap, using his finger to point to the words. Da, who had never learned to read, did not see the need of school and would never have allowed Robby to attend, but Miss Stone educated him well. He had read most of her books by now, and he loved them. "They will be yours when I'm gone," she had told him once. He had given a quick shake to his head. No, he did not want to think of Miss Stone's death. "Oh, don't fret," she had said. "I've no plans to depart soon." She had smiled at him. "Still I want you to know about the books. I haven't any family, and I want you to have them."

There had been no supper for him the night before, and shortly the smell of porridge forced him up.

Da did not appear until midmorning to demand Ma fix him something to eat. Robby stayed out of the kitchen until he heard his father go out the back door. He helped his mother carry the heavy laundry out to the backyard, and they were hanging up a sheet when Da appeared, red-faced with hurry and excitement.

"It's a good day for the Hares," he shouted as he came around the house. Robby glanced at Da and turned back to put a clothespin on his end of the sheet. He bent to take an apron from the basket, but his father grabbed his arm. "Listen to me, boy," he said. "I've got important news." Da leaned his head to point toward the house. "Inside with the two of you, I say. Let the laundry wait."

A great dread grew in Robby. Da took Ma's arm, and Robby followed. "I'll have me a cup of tea first." With an air of importance Da settled in his usual chair at the end of the table while Ma went to get his cup and the kettle. Robby moved from the doorway to the window. Da slapped the table with his hand. "Set yourself down, boy, you make me nervous with that blasted pacing about."

Robby sighed and went to the bench. Ma brought Robby a cup too, but he shook his head. She poured Da's tea and sat on the bench across from Robby. "All right, then," Da said after a long drink of tea. "I was out for a bit of a walk, and what do you think I see?" He looked from his wife to Robby. Neither of them spoke. "I see money, yes sirree, Bob, money just as plain as the nose on me face."

"You found money?" Ma asked.

"Well, not as much found it as found an opportunity to lay hands on it." He nodded his massive head in satisfaction. "I come around a corner and there is a funeral procession, a whole passel of people following a hearse drawn by four white horses."

Robby leaned his elbows on the table and lowered his head to rest in his hands. Da reached out to hit one arm. "Get your head up, boy. I'm talking here, I am. So, of course, I follows along to the grave site, then just slip away, all natural and easy. No need to watch the poor soul put down, seeing as it be me and my boy that will bring him back up this very night."

"I won't do it, Da." Robby's voice was low but firm.

The slap came as quick as a heartbeat, and the hand knocked Robby's head against his right shoulder. Jerking himself straight again, he repeated. "I won't do it."

The second slap was as fast as the first, but Robby knew it was coming. Bracing himself with his hands on the table's edge, he closed his eyes before the blow struck. He took in a great breath, opened his eyes, and said again, "I won't do it."

Then suddenly Ma was there, grabbing Da's arm. "Don't hit him again, Roger. I'll go with you my own self. You know my arms are strong, likely strong as Robby's. Just don't hit him again. I'm begging you, please."

Da turned to stare at her, then pulled his arm free of her grip. He turned back to Robby. "So you would send your mother out in the night to do your work, would you, little baby?"

Robby swallowed hard. "I'll go," he said almost in a

whisper. "I'll have to go." Da said nothing more, and Robby left the kitchen.

The rest of the day passed in usual fashion. He went back to hanging clothes on the line to dry. He pumped water and then walked to the market to buy cod for supper. Market Street was full of stalls where all kinds of food were sold. Vendors also roamed the street, their carts or baskets full. "Buy yourself a bit of a treat," Ma had said when she handed him the money for the fish. Robby knew she hated that he had to go to the cemetery again and wanted to make it up to him.

He did not want to decide too quickly what to buy. It was an unusual pleasure to spend a few pennies, and he had no wish to speed the process. He considered oysters, baked sweet potatoes, and peanuts, but a woman selling ears of corn drew him to her by the smell of her wares and by her cry, "Here's your nice hot corn! Smoking hot! Piping hot! Oh what beauties I have got!"

Robby sat on the ground to eat his corn and leaned against the trunk of a big tree, just beginning to leaf out. He told himself not to think of what lay ahead of him, but thoughts of the night's business could not be pushed from his head. His father would make him climb down into the grave again to fasten the rope to the body.

The corn was sweet and good, but Robby could take little pleasure in it. He finished the ear, wiped his hands on his trousers, got up, and headed toward a man who blew a tin horn and shouted, "Here comes the fisherman! Bring out your pan!"

He purchased the fish, slipped it into a bag his mother had provided for them and headed home, walking an extra mile, just as he had on the trip there, to avoid going by the cemetery.

All too quickly the evening passed. Da had himself a good sleep in preparation for their nighttime mission. From the kitchen where Robby sat by the stove, he could hear Da snoring. Ma came in to urge Robby to lie down. "You might be able to sleep some. Won't know for sure till you try."

He lay for a long time in the dark listening, his mind full of terrible images. He heard the town crier call out, "Twelve o'clock, and all's well." Some time after twelve he fell asleep.

Da woke him with a nudge from his boot. "Up, boy," he said. "It's well after two. We got to get moving."

Robby rubbed his eyes. He wished he could sleepwalk to the cemetery without knowing what he did, but he knew that wouldn't happen. Having slept in his clothing, he had only to take his worn jacket from the peg to be ready.

Da whistled as they moved along the cobblestones, Robby following with the wheelbarrow. A dog ran at them as if to bite, growling deeply at Robby, who paid it no heed. What did he care if a dog bit him? Da turned back and swung at the creature with his shovel, struck it, and sent it howling back where it came from. "What's wrong with you, boy?" Da asked. "That mongrel was about to bite you, he was, and you with a shovel in your wheelbarrow. Step to it, boy. You act like you ain't got good sense." Robby made no comment, and Da turned back to his whistling and his walking.

This time it was Da who led the way to the grave. "We're about to resurrect a rich man, we are." He stuck his shovel into the newly turned soil. "Pity is them doctors don't pay no more for a fellow as was well-heeled than for a pauper. Get that shovel moving, boy."

While he dug, Robby tried to tell himself that he was still asleep, that all of this was only a bad dream, but all too soon he heard the dreaded thud of his father's shovel striking the casket. "There we go. We'd better shovel off the whole thing. Won't be as easy getting a man out as last night's job."

This time Da had brought two crowbars and had placed them beside the grave. He reached for one and tossed it to Robby. "You pry at this end. I'll move down to the other."

Robby threw himself into the job. "Get it done and over," he told himself. Tomorrow he would gather his few belongings and leave his father's house. No matter how his mother begged, he would go, just start walking. Da would have to kill him to make him stop. The popping off of the casket's fastener made him stop dreaming of escape.

"Up with you, now," said Da, "and hand me the rope. This one needs pulling open."

Robby scrambled up and threw down the end of the rope. Da attached it well to the coffin handle, climbed out, and began to pull. "Grab hold," he yelled to Robby. "The thing is powerful heavy."

When the lid was finally open, Da untied the rope, made a big loop of the end, and handed it to Robby. "Down with you, boy, and mind you don't step on him. We cannot sell damaged goods. There's room for a foot on each side of the body. Then bend and get the rope over his head and around his chest."

"It's too dark, Da. I can't see him."

"Balderdash! That moonlight's bright as day. Down there, now!" Da took a step toward him.

Slowly, Robby lowered himself. The corpse wore a white shirt, making it easier to see. When he leaned over the body, a sickeningly sweet smell met him. He held his hand over his mouth and swallowed back the gorge that rose in his throat. This one had been dead too long before burial. Robby forced himself to lift the head and then one shoulder after the other, sliding the rope around the body.

"All right," said his father. "You'll be lifting on this fellow, way too heavy for just me. Get a good hold on him." Robby stepped carefully back, then put a hand under each of the dead man's arms. "Heave," yelled Da, and Robby did. Slowly, the body began to move. "Get a lower hold now," Da yelled, and Robby moved his arms to the waist, lifting the upper body to ground level. "I'll hold him here," Da panted between words. "Get yourself up here to help me."

"We can't get him in the bag," Robby said when they had laid the body beside the grave.

"No, we cannot. Just never figured how heavy a dead weight could be, and me with nothing but a scrawny boy for help." Da took the bag from the wheelbarrow. "This fellow ain't even particular big for a growed man." He shook his head. "We'll get his top half in the cart and leave his legs dangle over. Just hope we make it to the school without some busybody snooping about. Help me get his clothes off."

Robby started with the shoes, but he had to stop and vomit. "Get hold of yourself, boy," Da said. "Your mother's coddled you, that she has. Stop acting like a little girl."

"Say what you want to me, Da," he thought. "It won't matter after tomorrow. After tomorrow, I'll be gone."

When the body was in the cart and the clothing thrown

back into the coffin, they covered the grave. Robby spread the white sack over the man, and it hung down over most of his legs. "Off with us now," said Da, "likely you'll have to spell me some on the pushing. Maybe I'll look for a fellow to team up with us, if I can find someone I'd trust. Don't go thinking you'll get out of the business, though, no sirree, Bob. Hare and Son, that's the name of this here resurrection business."

At the school, Dr. Bell was surprised to see them. "Back so soon?" he said when he came to answer the knock. He lifted the bag to look at the body.

"You want him or not?" Da folded his arms.

The doctor hesitated only a second. "Never said I didn't. You'll have to push the cart in." He led the way to the same room they had entered last night. Robby hovered near the door, afraid Ruth's body might be still on the table, all bloody and cut. When he saw that the table was clear, he stepped inside and moved to the chart, anxious for another look.

The doctor helped Da lift the body from the cart onto the table. In the dim light, Robby leaned close to the drawing to read the names of the organs. Then his gaze fell to a small table just to the right. A clear glass full of liquid held a grayish pink, roundish object with many ridges and grooves. Robby studied the object, then looked back at the chart. "Is that a brain?" The words came out without his thinking and immediately he was sorry.

The doctor did not seem to mind. "Yes," he said, and he stepped to a wash pan where he washed his hands. "Would you like to hold it in your hand?"

"No," Robby said quickly, but he was surprised that down inside himself he could feel the desire to do just that. The thought came to him then that the brain might be Ruth's. Maybe that brain was all that remained of the little girl who had worn the white dress. He edged away from the table and toward the door.

The doctor paid Da and led them back to the front door. "When a child is six or so, the brain is as large as it will ever be," he said to Robby after he had opened the front door.

Robby nodded. He was never going back inside that place, but something made him turn back for a second to see the light in the window.

At home Robby heated water on the big black stove. "What are you doing?" Da demanded from the table as he ate bread and butter.

"I want to wash myself before I go to bed," Robby said, and he shuddered. Did the smell of death cling to him or was it his imagination? Either way, there would be no rest for him until he was clean. Tomorrow he would start a new life, and he would wear clean clothing, not even bothering to take the things he now wore with him.

CHAPTER THREE

The next morning Robby began at once to plan his escape. In the closet beneath the front stairs was an old valise that had belonged to Ma's uncle, who once lived in the house. He would take his other change of clean clothes, brought in from the clothesline just yesterday, fold them, and when he could go into the closet unobserved, he would deposit them in the bag.

His plan was changed by a loud knock on the front door just as they finished breakfast. Ma hurried to answer. "Have you rooms to let?" Robby heard a man's voice ask. "I am in need of two, one for me and one for my daughter, Martha."

Robby pushed open the swinging door to stand in the doorway between the kitchen and the parlor. "We do indeed have rooms," Hannah Hare said. "Won't you come in?" Ma followed a small pale-skinned man into the parlor. He removed a tall black hat from a head covered with black hair. His eyes were black too, and seemed odd against his pale skin. His large, twisted nose and narrow lips made his face decidedly unpleasant. He held his hat in the same hand as a walking stick made from a rich dark wood with a handle of gold, and he moved with the manner of a man accustomed to receiving respect. Robby thought he looked out of place in the Hare parlor, with the red settee worn shiny by use, the lumpy, over-stuffed brown chair, and scarred wooden table.

Da got up from his breakfast and leaned around Robby. After he had a glimpse of the man, Da walked into the parlor. Ordinarily Da would pay no attention to the lodgers, only their money. He must think this man might be important. He held out his hand, but he dropped it when the man did not take it. "Welcome to me home," he said. "I'm the landlord here. Roger Hare's the name."

"Pleased to make your acquaintance. My name is Burke, William Burke. Could you show me the rooms, my good fellow? I am in something of a hurry, having left my young daughter at the train station while I search about for lodging."

"Yes sirree, Bob!" Da flashed a smile. "Right this way." He led the guest back into the hall and up the stairs. Robby could hear their feet on the stairs, and the sound of his father's booming voice. He stayed holding the swinging door until his mother went back into the kitchen, then followed.

Ma began to clear the dishes from the long, wooden table with its red checked oilcloth. "Your da's all excited because this Burke looks like a gentleman," she said, and frowned. "Me, I'd sooner have a common-looking lodger, one who ain't used to having fancy food."

Robby reached to gather the cups. "Ma," he said, "you've no call to fret. Why, you're the best cook in all of Philadelphia.

Everyone says so. Let's just pray this man takes the rooms. With two rooms rented, surely Da won't make me go back to the graveyard."

The dishes had just been stacked for washing when they heard the men come back down the stairs. Da pushed open the swinging door and stuck in his head. "Come in here," he demanded. "We've got ourselves two fine boarders," Da said when Robby and his mother were in the room. "Yes sirree, Bob. It's mighty proud we are to have you," he said, and he reached out to clap a hand on Burke's shoulder.

Burke stepped away and brushed at his coat where Da's hand had touched. "I don't care to be touched by those outside my family. Please remember that in the future," he said, frowning.

Da looked as if he had been slapped, and for a moment Robby actually felt a bit sorry for his father. "Sure thing, Mr. Burke, sir," Roger said. "When will you be moving in?"

"Right away." He turned to Ma. "The rooms do seem to be in order, but they want dusting. I trust you can take care of that immediately." He did not wait for an answer. "Who lives in the third room?" he asked.

"Miss Stone," said Robby's mother. "She is a dear old lady, and very quiet. She takes most of her meals in her room. She's not strong."

"Would you like the third room?" Roger asked. "Because if you do, that can be arranged."

Robby, who had stayed near the doorway, gasped, but no one seemed to notice. Would his father really turn out Miss Stone? She had been with them for as long as he could remember, and Robby knew she had no other place to go. If his father forced her out, Robby would find her another house where she could rent a room. He would find such a place even if he had to walk every street in the city.

"No," said Burke, "two rooms are all we require. I shall go now and fetch my Martha. We have traveled far, and she will be glad of a bed on which to rest."

"Off with the both of you," said Da as soon as the door closed behind Mr. Burke. "Get your dust rags and run. You've got to be on top of things in the place now that we will have a gentleman in the house. No more lazy lounging about for the two of you."

Ma's face turned scarlet and Robby knew she was thinking that it was Da who did the lounging about. He was afraid that his mother might not be able to keep her tongue, and then, of course, Da's famous temper would erupt. He was relieved when she, without speaking, took two pieces of cloth from her rag bag and handed him one.

They said nothing until they were upstairs, but just before they parted, each to tidy a separate room, Ma spoke. "He gives me the willies, that Burke does." She shook her head. "Mark my words, we will be sorry of his coming. I know we will."

Robby's eyebrows went up with surprise. "No, Ma," he said. "This is a lucky day for us. There will be no need now to go to the graveyard." He whistled while he dusted.

True to his word, William Burke returned soon after the dusting was finished. Ma had gone back to do the dishes, and Robby had taken his dust rag into the parlor. This time Burke did not knock. Robby heard the outside door open in the hall and looked up to see their new boarder come in. "I won't be knocking at a house where I pay to lodge," Mr. Burke announced, and he set down his bag. A girl followed him inside and stood beside him, her eyes down. She wore a brown cape that seemed too heavy for the spring weather. She was smaller than Robby, but he thought she looked to be about his age. Probably she had inherited her small frame from her father. She had not, thank heavens, inherited his looks. Her fair hair framed a face with fine, perfect features, and her skin was so clear that a light seemed to come from beneath it. She looked, Robby thought, like a china doll that should be kept on a shelf because it was not strongly made.

Robby realized he should respond to Mr. Burke's comment. "Certainly, sir," he said. "We'd not expect you to knock. Can I help you with your bags?" He leaned around the doorway to see if there were more bags in the hall. "Do you have more?"

"No," said Mr. Burke. "We traveled light. I expect we will be doing a deal of shopping once we're settled. What is your name, my lad?"

"Robert, sir, but I'm called Robby."

"Robby," said Burke, "this is my daughter, Martha." He reached out to stroke her blond hair. "Martha is not strong, and I shall expect you to be helpful to her when I am away at business."

"I will," said Robby, "I'll be sure to do that." He looked at the girl and smiled, but she continued to study the floor. Being helpful to this Martha might not be easy, but he would manage. These people had just rented two rooms, and taking care of this girl was a much better job than robbing graves.

Mr. Burke held out the bag to Robby. "Show Martha her room and take up the bag." He consulted a pocket watch. "I must hurry to a business appointment." He laid his hand against Martha's cheek. "You should rest yourself, my dear. I'll be back in time for the evening meal." He whirled about so quickly that the tails on his fancy black jacket flapped, and he was gone.

Robby, the suitcase in his hand, began to climb the stairs. The girl did not move, nor did she look at him. After a few steps, he paused and turned back to her. "Well, do you want to see your room now?"

She looked up and nodded. "Come along, then," he said, and he began to climb again.

At the top of the stairs, he paused and looked back at her. She moved slowly, staring at each step before she put her foot on it. Maybe the girl was not right in the head. She might be like poor Daft Jane. He hoped she was not weak-minded. If she was, she would need a great deal of watching, and Robby had no doubt the job would be his.

He opened the door to her room and carried the bag inside. Then he went back to the stairs to wait for Martha. She was about halfway up, but she stopped when she saw Robby.

"Come on up," he said, and motioned to her in case she did not understand the words. He waited for her. When finally she was beside him, he noticed that she breathed rather heavily. "This way," he said, and rejecting the notion that he should take her hand, he turned and went back into the room. It was not a large room, but Robby thought it a pleasant one. He took the girl's cape and hung it on a peg. There was a narrow bed, a washstand with a mirror, a small bureau, and in front of the open window was a little table with two wooden chairs pushed up to it. A fresh breeze made the clean white curtains lift.

"You'll most likely be comfortable here," Robby said. At just that moment, he heard his mother coming up the stairs.

Hannah Hare came into the room, her apron still wet from dishwashing. "Now isn't this fine. I see you children are managing quite well without me." She smiled at Martha, and Robby was amazed to see the girl return a lovely smile of her own. Ma moved to stand beside Martha. "Are you well, child?" she asked. "Your breathing seems a bit heavy."

Martha sighed softly. "We had typhoid, my mama and me. I got well . . ." Her voice broke. "Mama didn't get well."

Ma reached out to put an arm around Martha, who leaned into the woman's ample side. "Sometimes life is just terrible hard, and that's the truth." She turned the girl's body to face the bed. "You have yourself a bit of a lay down now, and Robby will come fetch you when the noon meal is laid." The girl did as she was told, and Hannah took the light blanket from the foot of the bed and spread it over her.

Robby followed his mother from the room, closing the door gently. "Poor little mite," she said when they were on the stairs, and she made a *tsk* sound with her tongue.

"Is she daft, do you think?"

"Mercy, no, just terrible tired and with a heart that's all in pieces. We'll be kind to her as we can be. She needs some kindness if ever a body did."

Robby thought that he had never known his mother to be unkind. He would be kind to her too. Still, this sad girl and her peculiar father were beginning to make him uncomfortable. He gave himself a little shake. The new boarders would keep him out of grave robbing. Nothing else mattered, did it?

. . .

At noontime, Robby went back upstairs to escort Martha to the kitchen. He was surprised to hear Miss Stone call to him through her open door just at the top of the stairs. "Robby, darling, come here, please."

He turned to go in her direction. The old woman sat in her rocker, and on the foot of her bed, Martha was curled up with a book of fairy tales by Hans Christian Andersen in her hand. Miss Stone motioned toward the girl. "As you can see, I've met Martha. Isn't it lovely to have her with us?"

"Yes, ma'am," Robby said, ashamed of the jealousy he felt. He did not want to share Miss Stone with this strange girl, but somehow it had already happened. She was in Robby's place reading his books, and she looked totally at home. "Ma's got vittles ready," he said, trying not to sound cross.

"Good," said Miss Stone. "Is your father home today, Robby?"

"No, ma'am, he isn't." He knew that the lady would go downstairs for the noon meal. She rarely ate in the kitchen if doing so meant eating with Roger Hare.

Miss Stone put down the mending she had been working on. "I believe I'm strong enough to go downstairs to eat." She rose and moved toward the door, calling to Martha, "Come dear, Robby's mother is a wonderful cook. She'll put some meat on your bones. You can be sure of that!"

"May I borrow the book?" asked Martha. "I'd like to read more."

"Certainly," said Mrs. Stone. "Take it to your room now."

When they were at the staircase, Robby took Miss Stone's arm. They moved slowly down the steps, Martha following. All the way down, Robby scolded himself for being jealous.

What if his mother sickened and died? What if he had no one left to him except Da? Well, at least Martha's father seemed a deal kinder to her than Robby's father was to him.

"Where did you last live, dear?" Miss Stone asked after they were all settled with full plates.

A nervous look crossed Martha's face. She started to say something, then paused. "Papa's family is all from Massachusetts," she murmured.

"That doesn't answer the question." Robby stabbed at the cake of butter with his knife. "She asked you where you lived last."

Robby's mother glared at him. "Ah, Massachusetts," said the old teacher at once, acting as if Robby had said nothing. "Do you know the story of the Pilgrims landing in Massachusetts?"

Martha shook her head. "You will soon," said Miss Stone. "I'll tell you all about them this very day."

Robby felt irritated. Martha had been allowed to get away with not answering a question asked her by her elder. Ma wouldn't put up with that from him. She had not answered the question about where she had lived before coming to their house. She had deliberately given an answer designed to stop other questions. What secret were Martha and her father hiding? He took a spoonful of beans from his bowl. He would find out.

All through the meal, Ma fussed over Martha, making sure her bread was buttered and her beans warm. The girl said no more than three or four words, and she barely looked at Ma or Miss Stone when they spoke to her. She did not look at Robby, not even once. Well, that was fine with him. Ma might not believe the girl to be daft, but Robby wasn't so sure.

When they had finished eating, Martha said, "I can help with the dishes." Her voice was very soft. "I do know what to do."

Ma refused. "That's very nice of you, but you should go read or rest. I'll have these things cleaned in a jiffy, I will."

Robby helped Miss Stone up the stairs, and Martha followed. "Thank you, Robby, my boy," she said when they reached her door, and turning to Martha she added, "I'll just have a little rest, and then I'll tell you all about the Pilgrims." She started through her door, but she turned back. "Robby," she said, "please come in for a moment."

She closed the door behind them and then said, "Robby, I hope you will be kind to little Martha. The child has a great sadness inside her."

"I don't think she's right—in the head, I mean."

Miss Stone laughed. "What makes you think that?"

"I don't know exactly." He shrugged. "She acts like she's afraid of us or something. Especially me."

"She's shy, that's all. Remember, everything here is new to her, and she may never have known a boy before." She sank down to sit on her bed. "Most of all, remember she has recently lost her mother. A child who has no mother feels very much alone in the world."

Robby began inching backward toward the door. "All right," he said. "I'll try being kind to her, if ever she gives me a chance."

"Does it bother you that I am letting her read my books?"

She slipped off her shoes, lay down on the bed, and motioned him to her. "After all, they are almost yours."

"I don't mind. Can she really read, you think, or does she just look at the pictures?"

"Oh, she can read very well. I asked her to read a passage from 'The Ugly Duckling' to me." She closed her eyes. "I am very tired these days. I told your father just yesterday that you are to have my books when I am gone to my rest."

Robby frowned and looked at the floor. "No, don't talk of such things. You won't die for a long, long time."

She smiled up at him. "I told him that my ancestors are famous for returning to haunt those who go against our last wishes." She laughed. "I told that father of yours that I would make him miserable if he tried to sell my books." She smiled again. "I think he believed me. I am quite a good liar."

Robby felt a lump rise up in his throat. Saying nothing more, he bent and kissed her cheek. She was asleep before he got to the door.

When he stepped out into the hall, he was surprised to see Martha standing in the open doorway to her room. "I've been waiting for you," she said, and he could see that she was very excited. "Please come into my room. I want to show you . . ." She did not finish the sentence. Instead she ran to the window and motioned for him. "Come quick," she said.

From the open window, the barking of a dog drifted to him. "There's a kitten down there," she said, and pointed. "I think it must be lost. That dog chased it up the tree, and now he keeps jumping up, trying to reach it."

Robby went to the window. The cat was small and yellow. "That dog lives down the street a house or two. Most likely he'll give up and go home before long," he said. He started to move away, but Martha reached out to hold on to his arm.

"Robby," she said, "I know you don't like me, but if you will just help me with the kitten, I won't trouble you ever again. I want you to help me get it and bring it into the house."

Robby pulled his arm free. He would not confess his resentment over having to share Miss Stone and her books. "I've got nothing against you," he said. "It made me mad that you wouldn't answer Miss Stone's question, that's all." She said nothing, only dropped her gaze to the floor. He stepped away from the window. "You'd best forget the cat, though," he said. "My father would never allow a cat about. He'd likely break the thing's neck."

"But it would be my cat. I would keep it in my room and save part of my food for it. Please, at least go with me outside. I am afraid of the dog."

Robby took another backward step. "The dog wouldn't hurt you, but you better forget the cat," he said.

Martha's shoulders sagged and her eyes filled with tears. She turned away from the window. For a moment, Robby thought she had taken his advice, but then she went to the peg and removed her cloak. "I'm going out there," she said. "Maybe I can at least hold her for a while."

It was Robby's turn to sag. This girl was going to be a lot of bother, but he knew he'd better go with her. If she got even a scratch, the blame was sure to fall to him. "All right," he said. "Just to hold it, though." They went down the stairs, Martha moving much faster this time.

Maybe his mother would forbid the trip. He led Martha through the kitchen, where Ma looked up from her dishpan.

"Going out, are you? The fresh air might do you a bit of good, but, Martha, you won't need that heavy cape."

The girl clutched the edges as if someone might try to take the wrap from her. "I get cold," she murmured.

"Martha's got her eye on a kitten," said Robby. "I've told her Da would never allow a cat in the house."

"I only want to hold it. Poor little thing is all alone and likely very hungry." Martha started toward the back door.

"I've tried to convince my husband to get a cat; cut down on mice, it would." Ma shook her head. "The man is mightily against it."

Martha went out the door, and Robby followed. The Hare house almost completely covered the property, leaving only a small stretch of earth between the dwelling and the alley. There was a small bit of land where Ma had said her uncle once had a garden. She and Robby had decided in the winter that they too would have a garden. They would need to plant vegetables soon. The yard also held a clothesline for hanging laundry. Bits of grass poked up through the ground. Two trees grew in the yard, a large one near the house, the other, short and spindly, holding onto life near the edge of the property. Sitting on its lowest branch was the cat, with the dog still barking and jumping toward it.

"Get! Rags, go on home now." Robby waved his arms, and the dog tucked his tail between his legs and moved down the alley.

"You're likely to get yourself scratched if you try to touch it," Robby warned, but Martha paid him no heed.

He hoped the kitten would climb higher when Martha approached, but it did not. "Nice kitty," she crooned, "nice kitty, did that awful dog scare you?" Slowly she reached out a hand, and the cat allowed itself to be removed from the branch. For a moment, she held it out before her. "Isn't she pretty?" she asked.

"She is," said Robby. "That's why you must not take her in, or even encourage her to stay around back here." He paused for a moment, and then drew in a deep breath. "You may as well know the truth. My father is often a very cruel man. Sure, there are times when he doesn't seem so bad. I used to enjoy those times, and believed he had changed his ways, but I was little then. Now I know his decent spells won't last. He likes to hurt things that aren't as strong as he is . . ." His voice faltered, but he went on. "Me, my mother, small animals. I'm telling you, he'd kill that kitten." He snapped his fingers. "He'd kill it like that."

"Oh!" Martha shifted the kitten so that she could have a free hand to lay on Robby's shoulder. "How dreadful! It must be awful to be afraid of your own father. My father is always most kind to me, but I worry—" She stopped suddenly.

"What do you worry about?"

Martha looked distressed. "Did I say worry? I guess I misspoke, that's all."

Robby studied her for a second. She had almost told him something about her father. What? He reached out to stroke the kitten. "Let's see if my mother has a bit of food for her."

Ma was busy now making a sausage pie for the evening meal, and she pinched off a good-sized piece of meat for the cat. "Take her out back and feed her this. Then, Robby, you must carry the creature down the alley a block or so, and set her down. Your father could be here any time now."

"I know," he said. "Martha knows she can't keep it. We just want to feed it a little first."

Outside, Martha settled herself on an overturned washtub. She let the cat sniff the meat, and then put the kitty and sausage on the ground between her feet. It was small, even for a kitten, and it did not eat quickly.

Robby paced nervously, walking from one side of the house to the other, looking for any sign of his father. He wished that cat would eat faster. Finally, he could stand the tension no longer. He bent to pick up the cat and what was left of the sausage. "I'll give it the rest when I've deposited it a safe distance from here."

"Oh, I can't bear to watch you take her away." Martha stood and moved to the door. "I'll just go inside before you go."

"I'm doing this to save your life, cat," Robby said as he walked.

He walked several blocks to an area of town that had expensive houses. Behind a large white house with pretty green shutters, he set down the cat and her food. "You'll find a nice home here," he said, and he turned to run.

Martha sat about halfway up the staircase, waiting for him. "Did you leave her?" she asked, and he could see that she had been crying.

"That I did. I chose a beautiful home for her with a large backyard so she can play." He decided to add a bit of a lie. "I saw a lady come out and pick her up." He whistled. "That cat will be living on easy street now."

Martha took a white handkerchief from her pocket and wiped her eyes. "Thank you, Robby. You aren't like the boys who lived down the block from me at my old house. They were rough and mean. Once they threw stones at me."

"Where was your old house?"

"Oh," she said, and her eyes darted around the room. "North Carolina." Her face twisted with distress. "Yes, we came from North Carolina."

Robby felt certain Martha was lying. He thought of saying so, but it surprised him to realize how much he disliked seeing her troubled. He would let the lie go for now. "Oh," he said. "Is it nice there?"

She nodded. He felt as if she knew he was aware of the lie. "Oh, well," he said. "It doesn't matter where you came from; you're in Philly now. It's a wonderful city." She smiled at him, and her pale face seemed to come alive. Maybe it wouldn't be so bad, this watching after Martha. "Let's go read some fairy tales," he said. "We can take turns reading aloud."

For a time they lost themselves in the stories. It was Martha's turn and she had just begun to read about Thumbelina when Robby heard steps on the stairs. "Someone is coming up. Doesn't sound like my father—must be yours."

Martha jumped from her chair, put down the book, and ran through the open door. Robby got himself up from the floor. "Oh, Papa," he heard Martha say, "we've had a very good day."

Robby went out then. Martha still stood beside her father, his arms about her. Robby nodded in greeting and said, "Hello, sir."

Burke nodded back, and Robby studied his face. What was it Martha had started to say about her father? Something worried her, but she wouldn't say what. Well, the man was kind to his daughter, but Robby was pretty sure he was not a good man. Maybe his mother was right. Maybe they would be sorry that William Burke had come to the house with the broken stoop. Robby couldn't say exactly what it was, but something about the man seemed sinister, and Robby was afraid of him. He moved to step around father and daughter, but suddenly he stumbled. Burke had thrust his walking stick low and hard directly at Robby's ankle. He lost his balance, grabbing at the railing around the second floor landing to keep from falling.

"Papa, your walking stick," Martha said, and she reached out to touch Robby as if to steady him.

"Oh, beg your pardon," Burke said, and he pulled back his stick. "Must have slipped away. Accidents happen, you know. I am dreadfully sorry."

He wasn't, though. That walking stick had been close to Burke's own leg when Robby had started his move. It was no accident, but why would Burke do such a strange thing? He pushed down his anger, but he did not acknowledge the apology. "I'll just go down to the kitchen now and help Ma with supper," he said.

Actually, it was too early to peel potatoes or lay the table. He wondered what business Mr. Burke went to that allowed him to come home in the middle of the afternoon. Robby resolved to ask Martha when they were next alone.

CHAPTER FOUR

It was the next morning before breakfast when he had reason to wonder even more about William Burke. While Robby had taken food upstairs for Miss Stone, Martha and her father had come in and sat down for breakfast. Da was in the kitchen too. Robby's mother had asked him to empty a bucket of water left from early morning mopping. He had just opened the back door when suddenly the cat was there, slipping between his feet and running into the house.

"Oh," shouted Martha from her place at the table. "Robby, our kitty came back." Before anyone else had a chance to comment, she left the table and scooped the kitten up in her arms.

Da set his teacup down hard on the long board table. "What's this business, boy? You know full well I ain't about to tolerate some cat hanging about me."

Robby licked his lips, trying to think what to say, but Martha spoke up. "Excuse me, sir," she said, her voice shaking, "there will be no hanging about you. The kitty will be mine, and I will keep it in my room. You shall never have to see it."

Da shook his head. "Not possible. This is my house, and I make the rules for it. Scrawny cats be against house rules."

Robby glanced at Martha. Tears rolled down her cheeks, and she looked pleadingly at her father. "See here, Hare," said William Burke. "It appears we've a bit of business to work out between us. Could we talk in the other room?" He used his gold-handled walking stick to point toward the parlor.

Da frowned. "I've just begun to eat me mush, I have."

William Burke pushed away from the table and stood up. Despite his small stature, he looked menacing. "Now!" he said, and he walked from the room.

Amazingly, Da stood and followed him. Robby and his mother exchanged surprised looks. "Children," said Ma, "come eat your breakfast while it is hot. I'll have enough to warm for the men."

Martha came back to her place and held the kitten on her lap. Robby ate quickly, knowing there might be a great ruckus in the parlor, where the two men were talking. He was hungry, and he wanted to face the coming explosion with his stomach full. Martha took a few small bites, then began to spoon mush into her hand and feed the kitten. "I'm sorry, ma'am," she said to Ma, "but I'm too excited to eat. I do so hope Papa is able to convince Mr. Hare. I thought I shouldn't waste the food."

Ma shook her head. "I wouldn't count on it, dearie. My husband hates animals, and he is not a man for changing his mind, not a'tall." The room was quiet for a time, and then they heard the footsteps. The men were coming back. Robby held his breath.

Burke came in first, but Robby could read nothing in his

expression until he smiled at Martha and nodded his head. "You may keep your kitten, my sweet."

Da was just behind Burke. Robby was amazed to see his father's smile and it was a good-natured smile, not the leer he sometimes had on his face when he was pleased with some bit of cruelty he had just carried off. "Get us some food, woman," Da said, and he took his place at the head of the big table.

Mr. Burke held his hand up. "Nothing for me, my dear lady," he said. "I am late for business." He bent down to kiss the top of Martha's head. "Have a jolly time with your kitten, my darling." He made a saluting gesture in Robby's direction, then left the room.

After breakfast, Martha went to her room with her kitten. Robby helped his mother clear the table. They had to reach around Da, who sat smoking his pipe, never lifting as much as a saucer to help. Robby expected his father to make an ugly remark about the new boarders or threaten to kill the kitten while no one was looking, but Da was silent.

Was Ma wondering as much as I was Da's change in attitude? Robby did not expect her to ask, but sure enough, when the table was clear and the heated water was poured from the kettle into the dishpan, she wiped her hands on her apron and asked, "What was it made you change your mind about the kitten?"

Robby thought now his father would surely make a hateful comment. Instead, Da puffed up like a great toad. "As usual, I done what is best for me family," he said. "Turns out our gentleman tenant be well connected." He nodded his big head to accentuate his remark. "Renting them rooms to Mr. Burke might just be the beginning of very good things for me."

"What good things?" asked Ma.

"Not things you'd likely understand." He leaned back in his chair and folded his arms across his big chest. "You just make mighty sure they be comfortable here." He turned his head in Robby's direction. "Boy, get yourself upstairs and entertain that girl. She's to be kept happy. You hear me?"

"Yes, sir." Robby needed no urging to leave the room. Upstairs, he found Martha in with Miss Stone again. She sat on the floor, her kitten in her lap, while Miss Stone told her about the Pilgrims landing on Plymouth Rock. Robby had read Miss Stone's history books and knew all about the story, but he sat down beside Martha until the tale was over. "Well," said Miss Stone. "I'm tired now. You children run along and come back after I've had a bit of rest."

"I really knew all about the Pilgrims," Martha whispered to Robby in the hall. "I told her I didn't because I could see she wanted to tell me."

Robby smiled. "Miss Stone is a mighty fine person, isn't she?"

"Papa says she won't live much longer. He told me not to get attached to her." She frowned. "But I already am attached. Why do people have to die, Robby?"

Feeling proud to have her turn to him with questions, he thought for a minute before he answered. "Well, I suppose if no one died, the world would be too crowded soon, wouldn't it? But I'll tell you, I think your father is wrong about Miss Stone. I think she will be around a deal longer."

They were outside Martha's room now. "I have a cup and

ball," she said. "Would you like to play a game of toss?" He nodded and followed her inside.

Martha took a wooden cup from the bureau drawer. The cup was built on top of a handle with a ball attached to the cup by a heavy string. Robby had seen such a toy and knew the object was to toss the ball up and catch it in the cup, but he had never played with one. She handed it to him. "Let's sit at the table and play," she said. "You take a turn first."

Three times Robby tossed the ball and failed to catch it. "Keep trying," said Martha, "you'll catch on." On the fourth try, he caught the ball. "Practice a little more," she said, "and we will have a contest."

Robby caught three more balls. "This is jolly," he said.

"I wish you could have played with me at my old home. I had ever so many nice toys, but I had to leave them." She stopped suddenly. When she spoke again, she whispered, even though they were alone in the room. "I'm not supposed to talk about my old home," she said.

"Why?" Robby leaned across the table to be closer to her. "Why aren't you supposed to talk about North Carolina?"

For just a second a look of surprise crossed her face, but then she looked down and shook her head. "Don't ask me, please. I am awfully sorry I said anything."

"Never mind." Robby handed her the cup and ball. He hated the distressed look on her face. "Let's have the contest now," he said, and he did not mind at all when she won.

At noontime, Robby went into Miss Stone's room to take her downstairs to eat. "My da is not around," he said. "He's gone out early to the pub and is likely to stay all day."

She smiled at him. "Well, that's good now, isn't it? Not

only do you and your poor mother have a rest from him, but he will come home full of drink." She laughed slightly. "Roger Hare is the only man I've ever known who is nicer when he is drunk."

It was true. Robby always liked to be around his father when he came home from drinking too much. Sometimes he would be too far gone to do anything but fall into bed, but sometimes he would have had only enough to make him softer. A few weeks ago, he had come home after Robby's mother had already gone to bed. Robby got up from his pallet and cooked his father some potatoes. While Da ate, he talked to Robby about his life in Ireland as a boy. He told about his brothers, Robert and Patrick. "I'll never see their faces again," he'd said as he wiped his hand across his face. "Do you mind what I told you about your name?"

"I do," Robby had said. "You named me Robert Patrick for them both."

"That I did, that I did." He began to tell, then, about meeting Robby's mother for the first time, just after he got off the boat from Ireland. "She was a pretty lass," Da had said, "a real pretty lass before she got mixed up with the likes of me."

He had even patted Robby's arm as they sat together on the kitchen bench. "You're a good son, Robby. Yes sirree, Bob," he had said, and Robby had thought he might cry.

The next day he asked his mother why his father was so much more pleasant when he was drunk. She had been scrubbing the kitchen floor right after breakfast and had stopped to look up at Robby, her hand still in the bucket. "It ain't easy to explain, son. He wasn't so rough and hard in our young days, and he worked along beside me like he's not done in ages." She shook her head. "Things were hurtful for him, and him expecting life to be easy in America. He thought he'd earn lots of money and send for his brothers, but he wasn't able to hang on to the scant few jobs that come his way. Lolly dying seemed to sort of finish him off. He's angry at . . ." She paused. "I guess he's angry at the world, maybe God too. Lord only knows what would have become of us if my uncle Tim hadn't died and left this place to me." She rung out her rag and went back to scrubbing. "He don't like me being the one to hold our bodies and souls together, but he knows he can't do it." She shrugged her shoulders. "I'd say when he drinks, he forgets all his failures."

Robby threw himself down on to the bench and laid his head on the table. "I hate him when he hits you, Ma. I hate him so much."

"Ah, Robby, try not to be hating him. Hate eats at you something terrible, especially hating your own blood kin. Your da's not all bad, though sometimes it seems that way. Try to feel sorry for him, all that pain inside. Father Francis says we got to pray for him."

Tears rolled down Robby's cheeks. "But, Ma, why do we have to stay with him?"

His mother pulled herself up from her knees. "You don't, Robby. You're smart and soon you will be stronger than your Da. You can get away, son. Just bide your time, and you can go. Me, I can't leave him. I vowed in front of God, I did. Besides, I'd have nowhere to go. This place was left to me, but, of course, in the eyes of the law it belongs to your da." She rose and carried the mop water out the back door to dump it.

Robby remembered the helpless feeling he had experienced

that day, and it all washed back over him as he knelt beside Miss Stone's rocking chair. "So," he said, "Da's not likely to show up for noontide meal. I'll help you down the stairs."

She laid her hand on his arm. "You're a dear, but I believe not. I'm mightily tired today. Be a good boy and help me over to my bed."

Robby helped her to her bed and spread the blanket over her. When she was settled, he moved to leave the room. At the door, he paused and turned back to her. "I'll bring up some food," he said. "You can eat just where you are. I'll pull you up a mite in the bed."

She shook her head. "No, Robby, I'll be asleep before you could climb back up the stairs. I'm that weary." She closed her eyes.

"Very well," he said, "but Ma has made an apple pie. I'll put a slice away for you and bring it up later." She made no sound, and he tiptoed back to stand beside her bed. Yes, she was still alive. He could see the cover he had spread over her rise and fall with her breath.

Downstairs he was surprised to find William Burke sitting in the big brown chair in the parlor. He had pulled the curtain away from the window and was reading a newspaper. When Robby entered the room, he glanced up. "I shall require more light. I can barely see to read even in the broad daylight," he said, pointing to the lamps attached to the opposite wall. "I had no way to light them."

"There is no oil in them anyway," said Robby. "I'll get some from the kitchen. We just bought a can."

"Thank you, my boy. That would be most helpful."

Robby moved through the swinging door into the kitchen,

where his mother was putting the last touches on the meal. "Robby," she said, "butter the bread for me. I had no notion his highness would return for a meal at noon. It's lucky I am that I have some chipped beef. You and I mustn't eat any so there's plenty for the boarders."

"He wants oil for the parlor lamp," Robby told her.

"It will have to wait till after we eat." She set a big bowl of boiled potatoes on the table. "Is Miss Stone coming down?"

"No, she was really tired. I'll take her something later. I promised her a piece of pie."

"And she shall have one." His mother took one more look over the table. "Tell them I am ready," she said.

Martha had joined her father in the parlor. "Ma's ready for us to eat now," Robby said, and he held the door for father and daughter to go through to the kitchen.

"My, what delicious smells," said William Burke. He took his place at the end of the table beside Martha, who sat on the bench. "I am most fortunate indeed to have found a house where the lady is a master chef and where there is a fine young son to keep my daughter company." He smiled broadly at Ma and then at Robby.

"Thank you, sir," said Ma, and Robby wondered if his mother still felt uncomfortable with having William Burke in the house. As to his own feelings, he had no doubt. William Burke might hand out compliments and charming smiles until Christmas without changing Robby's mind. He had seen the darkness in Burke's eyes when he apologized for tripping him yesterday. The man had taken pleasure in the small act of evil, as if it gave him power. Robby had to hold hard to the table's edge to resist the shudder that threatened to pass through him. Once during the meal, he felt Mr. Burke looking at him. He raised his gaze to meet Burke's eyes. They were the blackest, coldest eyes Robby had ever seen.

Swallowing back his fear, he said, "What's the weather like in North Carolina now, Mr. Burke?"

"North Carolina?" Burke frowned. "I am sure I wouldn't know, having never been in the state. Why would you suppose I know anything of North Carolina?"

Robby shot a quick glance at Martha, whose face had grown pale. He shrugged. "Oh, I guess I was wrong. I thought Da said you came from North Carolina."

"Yes, you are wrong," he said. "Don't trouble yourself about where we are from. You would be certain to find the story rather dull." He stood.

"Oh," said Ma quickly, "we've a nice apple pie. You must have a slice before you go."

William Burke pursed his lips and looked at the pie with lowered eyelids. "I never touch sweets," he said, "but the meal was delicious." He turned to Martha. "I must go back to business now, my dear. You will be in good hands here with Robby and his mother, will you not?"

Martha nodded. Her father kissed the top of her head and left the table. Ma handed the child a saucer with a piece of apple pie. "Here, dearie," she said. "This will put some color in your cheeks."

Robby wanted to talk to Martha alone, but she begged to be allowed to help with the dishes, and Ma agreed. Robby could see that having the girl help made his mother uneasy. Doubtless she was imagining how William Burke might react to his daughter becoming a kitchen worker, but when the table was cleared Martha made an announcement. "I should tell you that I won't mention to Papa how I helped. Sometimes I don't tell him things because he has such a lot on his mind. No need to trouble him more."

Ma gave the girl a quick hug. Robby knew that his mother enjoyed being with Martha, and his mind went to his little sister. He hoped no one had opened Lolly's grave to steal her away.

After the kitchen was clean, Robby and Martha took a slice of pie up to Miss Stone. "Robby," she said when they were on the stairs, "I'm sorry I lied to you about North Carolina. I'm so glad you didn't tell Papa what I said. He would have been most unpleasant about it."

"Well, where did you come from?"

They had reached the top of the steps, and Martha, ignoring the question, moved quickly to knock on the door. There was no response. "She might be . . ." Martha broke off her sentence and bit at her lip.

"She must be sleeping soundly," Robby said quickly, and he pushed the door open, setting the pie on a table near the door. Miss Stone lay in her bed just as he had left her. They moved closer and Robby made a gasping sound. "I can't see her breathing!" He threw back the cover and put his hand on Miss Stone's chest. The movement he felt was slight.

Martha went to the washbasin. "I'll get a wet cloth," she said. "Cool cloths are nice when a person is sick." She came back to the bedside and spread the damp rag on Miss Stone's forehead. "Oh, look," Martha cried. "She's opening her eyes."

It was true. The eyelids fluttered, and the tired old eyes

opened. Then the lips moved, but the children couldn't hear what she said. Robby dropped to his knees and leaned close. "Robby, my books, I want you to have them," she whispered.

"No! You aren't dying. I brought you apple pie! Let me get it. I'll feed you bites."

"Maybe later," she said, and she closed her eyes again.

Martha was crying softly, and Robby could feel his own tears about to burst out. "I've got to get a doctor," he said.

"Does your mother have money for a doctor?" Martha looked about the room. "Or maybe there is a purse with money in it here somewhere."

Robby shook his head. "No, there's no money here. She has a tiny income each month, but the rent takes it all." He began to pace the floor. "We've got to think of something. My da keeps the household money, and he would never pay for a doctor."

"Neither would my papa," said Martha.

"Will you stay with her? I'll tell Ma to check in on you. I've got an idea where I might find a doctor to come for free. At least he seemed kind when I met him."

Martha pulled the rocking chair to the bedside. She sat in it and took the hand that lay limply on the bed. "I'll stay," she said. "Hurry."

Robby ran down the stairs, calling, "Ma, I've got to go. Got to get a doctor for Miss Stone."

His mother came from the kitchen, her arms dripping from the laundry she had been doing in the big tin tub. "Wait, son, your da would never pay for a doctor for her. You know he won't."

"I have an idea," he said, but he did not wait for her to answer. He was out the front door, running.

CHAPTER FIVE

The hospital seemed much farther away than it had during the trips with his father. Robby had to stop to catch his breath three times, but finally the big stone building was in sight. When he reached the door, he paused. Should he knock? Maybe the door was not locked during the daytime. He tried the knob, and it moved in his hand. He pushed through the door, yelling, "Dr. Bell, Dr. Bell, I need you!"

Two men came from one of the rooms. Both of them wore white coats. "See here," said one. "What are you up to? You aren't supposed to be in this building."

"The door wasn't locked." Robby moved to go around the men, but one of them grabbed his arm. Robby tried to pull his arm back, but the man held on. "I need to see Dr. Bell, please," he said, and then he yelled, "Dr. Bell, I need you!"

Down the hall a bit, another door opened, and out stepped the man Robby was looking for. "It's all right," he said to the men. "I know this young fellow."

"Very well," said one. "Perhaps you can explain to him that it is not polite to come shouting about without being properly invited." They did not wait for an answer, just turned and went back into the room from which they had come.

"Please come with me, Dr. Bell," Robby said. "My friend is dying."

Dr. Bell put his hand on Robby's shoulder. "What friend?"

"Her name is Miss Stone. She's a boarder at our house, and she is old and has no money." His voice shook. "My father won't pay, but I will work. I will work hard for you, doing anything."

"All right, Robby," said the doctor, and Robby felt honored that Dr. Bell had remembered his name. "You wait here while I get some things." When he came back, he carried a black bag. "Where do you live?" he asked.

Robby gave him the address. "It's a good distance from here," he said.

"We'll take a carriage. There's always one ready in the back." Robby followed the doctor down the long hall. Several doors were open, and Robby thought that at another time it would be interesting to see what the rooms contained, but he didn't even glance at them now.

Outside, a sturdy brown horse stood harnessed to a little black carriage. "Climb up," said the doctor. He opened a small door and settled on the seat, the reins in his hands. Robby did not take the time to open the door, just climbed over the low side.

When the horse began to clop down the street, Robby let himself lean against the back of the seat. He knew the ride would be quicker than his run had been, but he wished the doctor would urge the horse to run. Finally, they rounded the corner of his street. "There," said Robby, "the fourth house." He was climbing out even before the doctor pulled the horse to a stop.

While the doctor tied his horse at the hitching pole, Robby ran to open the front door. "She's upstairs."

His mother sat in the rocking chair. Martha had settled herself on the foot of the bed. Both of them stood when Robby came in, followed by the doctor. "This is Dr. Bell," he said. "He's come to help us."

Dr. Bell took out an instrument, put tubes connected to it in his ears, and held the other piece to Miss Stone's chest. "Her heartbeat is not strong," he said when he had removed the tubes. He shook his head. "I'm not sure there is anything I can do." He took a bottle from his bag. "Get me a spoon, please," he said, and Robby ran for one from the kitchen.

When he returned, Miss Stone lay with eyes closed on pillows Robby's mother had put under her shoulders and head to prop her up. Dr. Bell poured a spoonful of the dark liquid from the bottle. "This elixir might give you strength," he said to her, and he touched her lips with the spoon. "Open up now," he said, "and swallow this."

She did, and to everyone's surprise she said loudly, "That's terrible stuff. Are you trying to kill me?"

The doctor leaned close to Miss Stone. "Quite the contrary, madam. You take this medicine," he said, "and I'll come back to see you if you need me."

Her hand lifted from the bed to grasp his arm. "I've no money for you, doctor," she whispered.

"Don't fret about that. Robby has found a way to pay me." He turned to the boy. "Walk out with me, and I'll tell you what I have in mind."

Robby followed Dr. Bell down the narrow stairs and out the front door. The doctor unhitched the horse from the hitching post. "There's little I can do for her. Give her the elixir every four hours or so. She might show some improvement." He touched Robby's shoulder. "I'm afraid her death will come soon." Robby dropped his head and tears seeped from his eyes. The doctor went on. "See if you can get at least a little food and drink down her." He shrugged his shoulders. "Who knows, she might recover. I've seen it happen. I'll not charge for the visit, but I would like you to work for me anyway. There are lots of jobs around the medical school that you could take care of now and then, and, of course, I'll pay you."

A thrill went through Robby, but then he thought of his father. "Would you object if I didn't tell my da?" He bit at his lips. "I'd sooner not tell him about the pay. Do you think that's wrong?"

"No, Robby. It is not wrong. You come by the hospital whenever you get a chance." He climbed up into his carriage then. Robby did not stay to see him go.

Going back into the dark house from the sunshine made it hard for him to see. For a moment, he stood at the foot of the stairs in thought. It hurt to think of losing Miss Stone, and now he knew that the loss would likely come soon. He wiped at his eyes and took a deep breath. His job was to try to take the best care he could of her and to make sure she did not die alone. He began to climb the long dark stairs.

Robby and Martha stayed with Miss Stone. Once Robby thought of questioning Martha about the North Carolina lie, but the time did not seem right. When they heard Burke come in the front door, Martha jumped up. "I'd best run down to

Papa," she said. "It wouldn't do to have him know I'm in here with a sick woman. I'll come back when I can."

Robby passed the time reading. When there was not enough light through the window, his mother lit the oil lamp. She also brought his supper and a cup of broth for Miss Stone. Sometimes, when he spooned it slowly into her mouth, she would open her eyes. Most of the time, she said nothing, but she did give him weak little smiles.

He heard Martha and her father come upstairs after the evening meal to go to their rooms. Later he heard heavy steps on the stairs. He sucked in his breath. Da was coming. He put his book down and hurried to the closed door. Was there a lock? No, there was a small latch, but Robby knew his father would need only to lean against the door to force the latch to fail.

In the hallway, his father paused, and Robby prayed he would turn back. He didn't. The heavy steps continued, and then the door was open. Da stepped into the room. "Your ma says the old lady be real bad." He walked to her bedside and stood looking down at her.

"Da," said Robby, who still stood by the door, "I've got to stay with her."

Roger Hare turned and looked at his son. "Of course you do, boy. I ain't here to tell you no different."

Robby stared at his father. Was he drunk? He had not detected the smell of strong drink as Da walked by him. "Thank you," he said.

Roger Hare moved toward the door. When he was near Robby, he stopped and touched the boy's cheek, drawing his hand away quickly. "You're a good boy, you are, and I be knowing it. There's a deal more of your mother in you than there is of me." Then he was gone.

Robby went to the door, but his father was going down the stairs. He was surprised when Miss Stone spoke. "Glory be! There is a bit of decency in him after all," she said, and her voice sounded much stronger than before. For a long time Robby stayed by the open door, staring out into the dark hall. Then, encouraged by the strength of her speech, he uncovered the piece of apple pie he had left on the table and was pleased to get several bites down her before Miss Stone went back to sleep.

Before she went to bed, Ma brought Robby's pallet, pillow, and cover to him. Robby opened his mouth to tell her about his father's kindness, but something rose up in his throat. He found he could not speak of it.

He was about to lie down on his pallet when the door opened and Martha crept in. She whispered, "How is she?"

He told her about the broth and the apple pie. "She spoke earlier, and her voice sounded stronger," he added.

"I'll sit with you a while . . ." She paused. "I mean, if you want me to stay."

"Oh, I do," he said. "You take the rocking chair. I'll get one of the chairs from the table. Does your father know you are in here?"

"Heavens, no. He's fast asleep. I stood outside his door and heard him snoring away." She was quiet for a minute, then she spoke again. "My father is not a cruel man, not really. He does try too hard to protect me sometimes, but he really isn't cruel even though he's done things . . ." Her words trailed away.

Robby moved one of the two straight wooden chairs from the table to be close to the bed. "What things?"

In the lamplight he saw her shudder. "Things I can't speak of."

"What business does he go to each day?"

"I don't know, Robby, and that's the truth." She sighed deeply. "I'm sorry I lied to you about North Carolina." She paused for a moment. "We lived in Boston, but you must not tell anyone."

"What did he work at in Boston?"

Martha looked over her shoulder at the door. "He worked with my uncle. They had a shipping business. We lived in a big splendid house with a lady to do the cooking." She shook her head. "We had to leave there after my uncle died. Mama and I were so sick, but Papa said we had to go. He loaded us up in a carriage with blankets wrapped around us. Mama died in New York. Papa stopped just long enough to have her buried. Then we drove off and left her. Papa sold the horse and carriage, and we came here on a train."

Robby thought there must be more to the story. Why would Mr. Burke travel with a sick wife and daughter? He really wanted to hear it all. He could see, though, that Martha had no intention of giving other details. He would not make her uncomfortable by pressing her to tell. Maybe someday she would want to talk about it.

They were quiet for a while, then Robby said, "I had a little sister, and her name was Lolly."

"What happened to her?"

"She died two years ago. In the winter, she got a fever and

a cough. Da got her a doctor, but it didn't do any good." He stopped and looked at Martha. "She had hair like yours, yellow as sunshine. She was just six when she died. We buried her with her doll."

"Was your father mean to Lolly?" Martha asked.

Robby shook his head. "He never was, but he wasn't really hard on me when I was younger." He shrugged. "Maybe he would have started hitting her too if she had lived longer. Maybe it is better that she died because I am afraid I might have done something awful to him if ever I saw him lay a hand on Lolly. Losing Lolly made Ma and me awful sad, but Pa just got meaner."

They did not talk more. Martha dozed some in the rocker, but Robby was afraid to nap. Every so often, he spooned some elixir or water into Miss Stone's mouth, and he was able to convince the patient to take a few more small bites of the apple pie. When light began to show through the window, Robby shook Martha's shoulder. "You best go back to your room now," he said. "It's almost day."

Before long, Robby heard the front door open and close. Mr. Burke was gone. He went downstairs, where Martha sat eating porridge. Robby got himself a bowl, ate, and was thinking of getting another when a knock sounded on the back door.

Ma went to open it. "Jane," she said, "you've come at a good time. We've porridge to share."

"Is he here, the one that yells?" Jane leaned into the kitchen and looked all about.

"No, just Robby and me, and our new friend Martha," Ma said. "You can come right in and sit at the table." She was a sad sight, matted hair that had once been red and was now faded and dirty to the point that Robby couldn't say what color it would be called. There were big dark smudges of what looked like soot on her face, and she wore a brown dress that was torn and filthy.

"I'm terrible hungry," she said.

Robby had seen Daft Jane from time to time for as long as he could remember. He had heard it said that she was once normal, but that she lost her wits when her daughter died, and she did often mutter about a lost child. Others said she was born that way and that the baby she rambled about had never existed. They said she only took to the streets after her parents passed away. She mostly hung around in the business section of town, and could often be seen in the alleys, eating scraps that had been thrown away by taverns. She also begged for food and came to the Hares' door fairly often. "We're poor," Robby remembered his mother saying more than once, "but we aren't poor enough to ignore starvation in another human being."

Jane's words were often muddled, but she never failed to know each of the Hares. She took one cautious step inside the kitchen, then crossed the floor at almost a run. She stopped short when she looked at Martha. "Oh," she said, "her hair is like gold. I had a little girl with golden hair." Her face twisted. "I think I did." She moved closer to Martha, peering at her intently. "You're not my little girl, are you?"

"No," Martha said in a gentle voice, "I lost my mama, though. Just like you lost your little girl."

"Here, dear," Ma said to Jane. "I have a nice warm towel. You can clean your face and hands." Jane took the cloth and washed, then dropped it on the floor.

She sat down and watched Ma as she dipped up the hot porridge, and needed no urging to eat when the bowl was in front of her. "You're kind to me," she said around her second spoonful. Robby thought Jane seemed more sensible than she often did, but then she added, "I was chased by elephants on the way over here. Did you know there are elephants in Philadelphia?" She did not wait for an answer. "No," she cocked her head to one side. "I forgot, we aren't in Philadelphia, are we, Robby?"

Ma stood close to Jane. "You know," she said, "if you would let me take you to the Quakers, no elephant could hurt you, and you would not be hungry or dirty again."

Jane shook her head wildly. "No, I was in the almshouse, but I escaped. I won't go back. They hit me and locked me up in a room."

"You weren't at the Quaker house. The people there are much kinder. Do you remember that you told me your mother was a Quaker, and so were you when you were growing up? Do you remember that?"

Jane looked distressed. "I thought you were my mother."

"No, I am but your friend, but I would like to see you with a place to sleep at night."

"Well, I am glad you aren't my mother," Jane whispered, "because I wouldn't want him to be my father."

Robby knew Jane meant his father, who would yell at her to get out if he found her at their table. Jane was daft, all right, daft as she could be, but she had wits enough to dislike Da.

Jane ate her porridge and a large hunk of bread with butter quickly, all the time staring at Martha. "Can I touch your hair?" she asked.

Robby could see that Ma was about to protest, but Martha spoke before there was a chance for Ma to say anything. "I'll come and sit beside you so you can reach me easily." She stood and moved to sit on the bench on the other side of the table. Jane caressed her hair.

For a little while no one spoke. "Jane," Martha said after a bit. "Robby and I would like to take you to the Quakers. Would you hold my hand and walk with us there?"

"It's some distance, quite a walk, dear." Ma had just filled the dishpan with hot water. "Let me take you, Jane. Martha has not been well, and the walk might be too much."

Jane drew herself away from Ma. "No, I want to go with this little girl. I think she might be my little girl."

"No," Martha whispered. "I am not your little girl, but I will come to see you often."

"Martha," said Ma, "I'm afraid I can't let you go. Your father is coming back here for a noontide meal. I've no desire to be explaining to the man why you ain't here."

"It's early yet. Likely I'll be back." She shrugged her shoulders. "Should I happen not to be, just tell Papa you tried to stop me. I'll deal with him when I get home." She leaned to look at Robby. "Can you show me the way?"

"I can." He climbed from the bench, but he looked at his mother. "I was going to feed Miss Stone her porridge."

"Leave that to me, son." She frowned and shook her head. "It's Martha that troubles me now, her weak as that kitten yesterday and now traipsing off for such a walk."

Martha stood too, and held out her hand to Jane. "Don't fret, Mrs. Hare. We will be fine," she said, and she led Jane to the back door.

Ma sighed. "You surprise me, Martha. You're a determined little thing, and brave."

Martha laughed. "Not brave, but I do know to do right. My mother taught me that."

"She knows to do right," Jane repeated. "She knows to do right." Martha led her out, and Robby followed.

"Let me get you a shawl, child," Ma called from the back door, but Martha waved her away.

"The sun is warm," she called.

Jane held out one arm. "The sun is warm," she repeated.

Outside the iron fence around Christ Church burial ground, Robby pointed inside to a grave near where they stood. "That's Benjamin Franklin's grave. He was real important in starting our country, but his stone just says he was a printer."

"I know who Benjamin Franklin was, Robby." Martha sighed. "Do you think me stupid? I had fine tutors when we lived in Boston." She pointed to a nearby bench. "Let's sit and rest a bit."

When they were settled, Jane leaned toward Martha. "I saw Robby at a different cemetery," she said in a half whisper.

Robby bit at his lip. "She means St. Mary's Churchyard," he said. "I go there sometimes because that's where Lolly is buried."

"Not at night," said Jane. "You shouldn't go at night."

Robby stood. "We'd best move on if we're to be home by noontide."

They had walked another block when Jane stopped moving. "Don't go to the cemetery anymore at night, Robby, please."

Robby looked at Martha and rolled his eyes as if to say he had no idea what Jane could mean. "I won't," he said, trying not to sound impatient. "Now let's quit talking about graveyards and get some walking done. Martha, why don't you tell Jane about Benjamin Franklin's kite?"

By the time the story was finished, the hospital was in view. Jane stopped walking and tugged her hand away from Martha. "I won't walk that way, not in front of that place. They put me in chains there." Her face twisted in thought. "I can't remember when that was, but I remember the chains." Her face brightened. "Now I remember. My mother came, and she made them take the chains off." She rubbed at her wrist. "Do you know where my mother is?"

Martha stepped closer to Jane. "We won't let anyone put chains on you."

Robby had heard that mental patients were kept on the third floor, and he felt certain Jane's story about chains was true. "There's a medical school on the first floor," he said. "I'm going to work there, Jane, sweeping floors and such, but we aren't going into the hospital, not now." He reached for Jane's arm. "We'll just walk by really fast."

Martha leaned around Jane as they walked, and she studied the hospital. "I've thought about being a nurse when I grow up," she said. "Papa says that nursing isn't a fit job for a lady, but I disagree. Maybe I'll work in that hospital."

"You'll go against your father?" Robby was surprised.

"He'd give in." She laughed. "Papa almost always lets me have my way. I'm not sure about nursing. It is just an idea I had. I might want to be a teacher." She shrugged. "I just know I don't want to be what Papa wants me to be, a proper lady who stays home and does fancy needlework."

They walked on another block before they saw the little

girl across the street. She was small, probably about six. Her hair fell in yellow ringlets, and she stood with matches in one hand. "Oh, look, Robby." Martha grabbed his arm. "See her matches. She's just like the little girl in Hans Christian Andersen's story. I want to help her. Let's go over and buy some from her."

Robby shook his head. "I've no money," he said. "Besides, she's not going to freeze today like the girl in the story. Let's move on."

"I've got some coins in my pocket," said Martha. "You stay here with Jane. I'll be right back." She dashed across the busy street.

"She's a pretty little girl," said Jane, smiling.

Robby took her arm in a firm grip. It would not do for Jane to dart out into the street, trying to get a closer look at the little girl. Robby did not like to look at her himself. She reminded him too much of Lolly. She was about the age his sister had been when she died, but he could see that this little match girl was much thinner. She wore a big apron with pockets for her matches and the pennies she got for them. Her dress was shabby and, like the little girl in the story, she wore no shoes.

Martha was talking to the child now. Robby took Jane's other arm too, and he turned her away, toward the window of the butcher shop where they had stopped. "Look what's in this window," he said. "Isn't that the biggest goose you've ever seen? I wonder how many people it would take to eat a bird that big."

"I'm not hungry now," said Jane. "We just had porridge,

remember?" She strained against his hold. "I want to see the little girl."

Robby glanced over his shoulder. "No," he said. "We've no time to cross the street. Besides, here comes Martha."

"Her name is Dolly," Martha told them when she had made her way back. "She's a darling little thing. I'm going to ask Papa for some dollars, and I will bring them back here and give them to her."

They began to walk on. "Doubtless," said Robby, "she moves from place to place to sell her wares."

"No," Martha said, and she turned to wave at the child. "She told me she is always in this area."

Robby wanted to change the subject. He did not like to think of the child, so thin and so like Lolly, even their names so close. "Just another block," he announced, and soon they stood in front of a tall white house with a sign that read QUAKER ALMSHOUSE.

"The steps are too high," said Jane, and she edged backward, toward the street.

"They're not too high for us." Martha tugged slightly at Jane's hand. "Come with us, dear. We need to go inside."

When Robby knocked at the door, it was opened by a pretty lady. Her dress and bonnet were white, but she also wore a sort of apron made of light blue material. "My name is Robby," he said to the lady. "This is Martha." He touched Jane lightly on the shoulder. "And this is Jane. She needs a place to stay."

They stepped inside, and Robby noticed the lady slid a bolt back in place to lock the door. She introduced herself as Miss

Ferguson and led them into a small office, where she invited them to take chairs on one side of a small white desk. The lady sat behind the desk and took a piece of paper from the drawer. "Now, Jane," she said. "What is thy last name?"

Jane closed her eyes and pursed her lips. "I don't remember, but I know I used to have one. My mother told me about it, but she is in the cemetery now."

"Oh, I see." Miss Ferguson nodded knowingly. "Well, no matter, we will give thee a nice clean bed and find work for thee to do about the place."

"No chains." Jane folded her arms across her chest. "I don't like chains."

"No one is forced to stay in our house, but we do lock the doors." She looked at Robby and Martha. "We have others, too, who might wander out without meaning to leave."

"Oh, please stay, Jane," said Martha. "This house is so clean and bright. You will be safe here."

"Yes," said Jane, "clean and bright."

Miss Ferguson stood. "Say good-bye to thy friends, Jane, and we shall start with thee having a nice warm bath." She rang a small bell, and a girl came into the room. "Show these people out, Tillie." She turned to Martha and Robby "Thank thee for bringing Jane to us. Please feel free to visit us on Sunday afternoon if thee would like to do so."

"Oh, thank you, Miss Ferguson," said Martha. She kissed Jane's cheek. "We will visit you, Jane. We will." Tillie led them to the door, and outside they heard the bolt slide back into place.

Robby looked up at the sun. "It's awful near to noon," he said.

"I saved a few coins." Martha touched her pocket. "I'm not sure they are enough to take a trolley."

"There's a trolley track just one street over," Robby said. "Let's hurry."

They turned at the corner and covered the block quickly. A trolley car pulled by two big horses had stopped on the next corner. "That's just enough for one fare. Do ye have nothing more?" the driver asked when Martha gave him her money. Martha took a step backward, but Robby stopped her.

"You ride," he said. "That way you will be home before noon. Tell Ma I'm coming."

He watched the trolley pull off, then turned to walk away. He had not gone far when he saw her. The little match girl had taken a new position on the edge of the street, as if to cross when the chance came. What came, though, was a runaway horse, black with reins flying loose. It came fast, so fast there was no time even for a scream.

Robby saw the horse run into the girl, knocking her onto her back and racing away. A lady and a gentleman came to kneel beside the child, and Robby bolted toward them. "Dolly," he called. "Dolly, are you hurt?"

The man gathered the child into his arms. "Are you her brother?" he asked when Robby was beside him.

"Yes." The word was out of his mouth before he could think.

"She's breathing, but she's unconscious."

"We've got to get her to the hospital," said Robby. "We've got to get her to Dr. Bell."

The lady had already flagged down a coach. "Take this child to the hospital, please," she called to the driver, and she ran to open the door for the man, who laid Dolly on the empty seat. Robby scrambled in and onto the other seat.

"Thank you," Robby called through the open window as the coach pulled away. He drew in a long breath. Then he dropped to his knees to be closer to the little girl, taking her hand between both of his. "Dolly," he said. "Dolly, please wake up."

Her eyes fluttered, but they closed again. She moaned. "I'm hurt. Hurt so bad."

"Just hang on," Robby said. "Hang on and Dr. Bell will help us."

At the hospital, the driver hopped down. "I'll get the child," he said, and Robby was glad. He could have carried the thin body, but it was better for him to run ahead for the doctor. The driver followed him to the big wooden door on the first floor. Robby had not even thought that it might be better to take her upstairs.

The door was unlocked, and Robby shouted, "Help," as soon as they were inside. Dr. Bell came from one of the classrooms. "A little girl," Robby called. "A horse ran into her."

"Take her to the surgery." He motioned for the man to follow him to the fifth room. "Put her on the table," he said, and the man did.

"We will be a-praying for your sister," the driver said before he went out the door, and Robby thanked him.

Dr. Bell lighted the big lamps. "I was about to leave. We let the students go early today. Is this your sister?" he asked when he was beside the table again.

"No." Robby shook his head. "They thought so, but she's

not. She was selling matches on the street. Her name is Dolly. Please fix her, sir, please."

"Dolly?" the doctor said. "Dolly, can you hear me?"

She did not open her eyes, but her lips moved. "Hurts," she whispered. "So bad."

The doctor took her hand. He leaned close to the girl's ear. "Show me," he said, and he laid her hand on her abdomen. "Show me where it hurts, Dolly." His voice was low, but insistent. "Show me with your hand."

Dolly moved her hand to her left side. "Here," she managed to say.

Dr. Bell's fingers moved over the spot, and he pressed once. Dolly screamed. "Likely it's her spleen. Robby, run upstairs and tell the woman at the desk that I need a nurse and some ether. I've got to operate." He moved to the steel basin and began to wash his hands.

Robby flew out the door and up the stairs two at a time. Once his foot missed slightly, but he grabbed at the rail and did not slow down. At the top of the stairs, he saw two women in white smocks behind a counter not far from the front door.

He opened his mouth to shout, but the run had depleted his breath, and he had to rest for a second before he called, "Dr. Bell sent me for a nurse and ether. He's got to operate." Without waiting, he turned and ran back. Downstairs, he was surprised to see one of the women step into the hall, a large glass container in her hands. On her arm were several cloths. She moved to room five, slightly ahead of Robby.

"How did you get here so fast?" he asked.

The woman did not slow her pace. "There's an elevator

back there." She leaned her head backward slightly. "It is for use by the staff only."

They were at the door now. Robby did not turn back to try to see, but he would look for the elevator another time. He had heard of them but had never seen one.

"Nurse Bigbey," said Dr. Bell. "Good. Give me the ether. I'll use it while you scrub. Robby, you wash up too. In case we need you."

The doctor poured the ether into a small steel bowl and soaked a heavy cloth in it. The smell filled the room, and Robby, washing his hands, thought for a moment that the smell would make him vomit. He swallowed and willed himself not to be sick.

A small table holding a tray with sparkling instruments now stood beside where Dolly lay. "Robby, stand on the other side, and don't move unless we say so. You can hold her hand if you want." Dr. Bell laid the cloth over Dolly's closed lips and nose. "She's unconscious again, but we need to make sure she stays that way."

After a time he moved the cloth away, threw it on the table, and held out his hand. Robby watched the nurse put a knife with a long thin blade into the doctor's hand. He did not watch the cut.

He closed his eyes and prayed, "Please, God, let Lolly live." Even when he realized he was thinking of the wrong name, he did not change it. Doubtless God knew who he meant, and the name went so well with the prayer.

The room was quiet until the doctor spoke. "Yes, it's her spleen. Sponge. I think I can repair the injury. I've got to soak up the blood and close the wound."

Robby let his eyes flit open for a second, and he saw the doctor working on a purplish organ, soaking up blood. He closed his eyes again. "I'm ready to sew it up now," the doctor said, and after a few minutes he added, "Ready to close now."

Robby, still praying, opened his eyes to see Dr. Bell with a big needle and thread, sewing the incision closed while Nurse Bigbey used sponges to stop the bleeding. Suddenly, Robby's knees went weak, and fearing he would fall, he moved away from the table and sank into a straight-backed chair near the wall.

"She will be asleep for a long time," said the doctor. "Do you have any idea where this child lives, Robby?"

"I don't." A sudden frightening thought came to his mind. "I don't think her family could have much money."

"We do not turn away people because they are poor here, not in Philadelphia." The doctor put down his needle. "You go on home, Robby," he said. "We will get this child upstairs and into a bed. You can see her tomorrow if you want. By that time, I hope she will be able to tell us where she lives."

With a great effort, Robby pushed himself up from the chair. "Will she be all right?"

"I hope so, but we won't know for a while. I think I've repaired the spleen. Now we have to worry about infection." Robby saw the nurse pour medicine on a large cloth and begin to wipe at Dolly's stomach where the doctor had cut her.

"Wait, Robby," Dr. Bell called just before Robby opened the door. The doctor came to him, put his hand into his trouser pocket and pulled out some coins. "Take a trolley home." He put the money in Robby's hand. "You're far too tired to walk that distance."

"Thank you, sir. Thank you from me and from . . ." He paused, concentrating hard on the name. "Thank you from me and from Dolly." The doctor smiled and touched Robby's shoulder as he left the hospital.

"Robby," Ma shouted when he came in the back door, and she jumped from her rocking chair. "We was worried about you, powerful worried. Where have you been?" Martha was there too, with the Hans Christian Andersen book open on the table where she sat.

"I've seen a marvelous thing," he said. "I've seen Dr. Bell do a surgery. I've seen him save a life." His voice was low and full of wonder, and he told them every detail of the story.

Martha gasped when he told of the horse running wild into the little girl, but neither she nor his mother spoke. They leaned toward him, listening, until the story was finished.

"I was just reading 'The Little Match Girl' to your mother," said Martha when he stopped talking. "May I go with you tomorrow to see her?"

"What would your father say about that?" Robby looked over his shoulder toward the parlor door. "Where is he now?"

"Gone out," said Martha.

"And your da too?" said Ma. She went to the stove to get a plate of food from supper. "You missed two meals, must be starved."

"Did Da go with Mr. Burke?"

"No," said Ma. "Doubtless your da is at the pub."

Robby looked at Martha, who shrugged. "Papa's gone off to his business," she said. "I don't know what he does."

Robby was glad the men were gone. The house was peaceful

and friendly. "You should see how Martha managed Jane, Ma," he said while he ate. "It was pure a sight to see."

Ma put butter on bread for Robby and looked over at Martha. "It's a gift, sweetheart. One God means you to use."

Martha's cheeks flushed slightly with embarrassment. "We mustn't mention anything about Jane to Papa," she said. "He tries too hard to protect me."

After he had eaten, Robby went up to say hello to Miss Stone, but found her sleeping. He went back downstairs, laid out his pallet, and fell immediately to sleep.

CHAPTER SIX

The next morning Ma stood at the stove scrambling eggs when Da came in. Robby did not meet his father's eyes. There had been no communication between them since those moments of unusual kindness on Da's part in Miss Stone's room. Robby was far more accustomed to his father's anger and did not know how to react to any kindness from him.

Da went to the stove to look into the skillet. "Smells good," he said, "and you've made a big batch. Our lodger is a small fellow, but he can put food away." He glanced quickly at Martha, who had just come into the kitchen. "Not that I begrudge the man a bite, no sirree, Bob, not a bite."

Mr. Burke came next through the swinging door, and he smiled at Robby. "Smile back," Robby told himself, "act normal," but, remembering the walking stick between his feet, he felt a shiver go up his spine, and he wondered again what business Burke went to each day.

"Papa," said Martha when they were all settled at the table, "yesterday Robby saw a little girl who sells matches get injured by a runaway horse. He took her to the hospital and watched the doctor do surgery on her. Isn't that amazing?" She turned her gaze to Robby. "What was the body part they fixed? I can't remember the name."

"Spleen." He put his hand to the left side. "It's right here, kind of behind the stomach. I don't know what it does, the spleen, I mean, but I want to find out."

Mr. Burke curled his lip in a sneer. "Really, Robby, I don't care to have discussions of body parts with my breakfast. Besides, the poor little urchin would have been better off left to die."

Martha gasped. "Papa, how can you say such a thing?"

"I only meant, dear, that the child must have a very hard life. It might well have been a kindness to shorten it."

"Well," said Martha, her cheeks burning with anger, "I don't think so."

"Me neither," said Robby. Without saying anything more, he took his plate and went to finish his eggs on the stairs. He was still there when Martha came into the parlor to say good-bye to her father.

"I really am sorry for upsetting you, my dear," said Burke. Evidently he had already apologized once, and Martha must have announced her plans to visit the child. "You know I could never be unkind." Robby, listening from the stairs, had to fight the urge to cry out in protest. Burke took his wallet from his pocket and pulled some bills from it. "Here," he said, handing Martha the money. "You and Robby should ride the trolley to the hospital. Buy all the child's matches from her. You can give them to the Hares."

"Thank you, Papa," Martha said, and she kissed him good-bye.

After the man was gone, Robby came down the stairs and went into the parlor. "Oh, look," Martha said. "Papa left his walking stick."

"I'll go catch him," Robby said. He grabbed up the stick and ran. "Tell Ma I might be gone for a while," he yelled over his shoulder. Outside, he could easily see William Burke at the end of the block, but he did not hurry or call out to him.

The stick was a perfect excuse to follow the man. He was determined to see what business Burke went to each day. On the second block, Robby could not see him. He moved slowly forward and was in front of two buildings with a small space between them when suddenly Burke stepped out to stand in front of him.

"I don't like to be spied on, Robby," he said coldly. "Of course, I am glad you brought my stick, but I wonder why you did not call out to me earlier." He laughed, and it sounded to Robby less like mirth than evil. "I knew you were behind me. Don't try to outwit me, my boy. You will fail."

Robby stood, unable to think of a response. Just before Burke grabbed the stick, Robby's eyes fell on the handle. Engraved in the gold top was the name "Jacob Taylor." Robby looked away quickly, but he felt Burke's eyes on him, felt Burke's knowing what he had seen.

Burke smiled. "I am quite attached to my stick. I've no need to lean on it, but I like to have it with me for protection." He touched the gold handle. "I dare say I could kill a man with one blow over the head with this, should it ever prove necessary to resort to such violence."

Again, Robby could think of no reply, and anyway, his mouth had gone too dry to speak. He nodded and stood absolutely still as he watched William Burke walk away. Who was Jacob Taylor?

Robby knew this was his chance to follow, but he could not move. His eyes strained to watch as long as he could see the man, then he turned back. When he got home, Martha was in her room feeding her cat from an old cup Ma had given her. "Did you catch Papa?" she asked when she saw Robby at the door.

"I did," he said. "Did you know the name Jacob Taylor is on his walking stick?"

She looked down and began to stroke the kitten that had come to sit on Martha's lap. "I had forgotten about the writing," she whispered.

"Is Jacob Taylor your papa's real name?"

"No, the stick already had the name on it when Papa got it." She put down the kitten. "Why are you always asking me questions? Let's get ready to go to the hospital."

Robby felt anger rise up inside him. He thought he and Martha had become friends, but he knew she was not telling him the whole truth about the stick. He'd had enough of the girl and her secrets. "I'm not supposed to ask you anything about a man who lives in my own house? Well, I'll tell you this: I intend to find out what business he goes to each day, and if it is not honest work, I'll go to the police about it!" He stepped back out of the room and slammed the door. In the hallway, he stood quietly and listened. He could hear Martha's sobs. Well, he told himself, let her cry, but before he was down the stairs, she called to him.

"Wait, Robby." He looked back to see her leaning over the upstairs rail. "I'm sorry I was cross with you."

His anger drained. Poor thing, it must be terrible for her, having Burke as a father and her with no mother. Da was not the best father in the world, but he was a dozen times better than William Burke.

"I'm sorry too," he said, and he turned to go up again. "Let's see Miss Stone before we go."

They found her sitting in her rocker. "I ate every bite of the breakfast your mother brought me this morning," she said, and Robby could see that she looked much stronger.

They told her then about Jane and about little Dolly. "Oh, Robby," she said, "what a wonderful experience for you, watching a doctor save a life!" She paused for a second, thinking. "The spleen, ah yes, that is an organ that helps filter our blood, and it helps us fight infections too. I am glad they did not have to remove the little girl's."

After the good-byes were said, Robby and Martha were out on the street again and enjoying the nice day.

"I wonder if anyone ever caught that runaway horse," Martha said when they were seated on the trolley.

The memory of the animal's speed flashed through Robby's mind. He shrugged. "I don't know, but if they didn't, he's certain to be far from Philadelphia."

At the hospital, Robby led Martha to the big front steps, feeling rather proud of knowing his way about. "They have an elevator here," he said. "Have you ever been on an elevator?"

Martha shook her head. "Me neither," he said. "This one is for doctors and nurses to ride, not regular people, but I mean to see it when I start work here tomorrow." The place smelled strongly of medicine and of the polish used to make the wooden floors shine.

At the big counter, they asked to see Dolly. "Are you Robby?" the nurse asked.

"Yes."

"Dr. Bell said you would be here and that we are to let you see the child, but only briefly. Follow me." She smiled. "You may bring your friend. Do not go near the patient, just step inside the curtains for a moment."

They followed the nurse into a big room with curtains around beds. One curtain was open, and an old woman sat up in the bed. "Come see me, children," she called, but the nurse shook her head.

About halfway through the huge room, the nurse stopped. A woman sat in a chair just outside the curtain. Her dress was shabby, but her face was pretty. Robby could see that she looked like Dolly. "This is Dolly's mother," the nurse said. "The child was able to tell us this morning where she lives."

The woman stood. "Are ye Robby?" A big smile covered her thin face. "The doctor said you saved my little girl, getting her here so quick-like. I'm obliged to you, ever so obliged."

The nurse pulled back the curtain for Robby and Martha to step inside the cubicle. Dolly was asleep, but her skin no longer looked like chalk. "She looks better," Robby whispered. He wondered if she had been able to eat anything, and he asked the nurse.

"Too soon," she said, "but by this evening we can give her broth. She's going to be all right, we believe." She pulled the curtain closed. "You two should go out quietly now," she said. "I am going to tend to another patient." She hurried away.

"I have something for you," Martha said to Dolly's mother, who had sat back down, and she took the bills from her pocket. "My papa wanted you to have this," she said, and she laid the money in the woman's lap.

"Oh!" Tears spilled from the woman's eyes. "Thank you for bringing this gift, and thank your sainted father for me too."

"I will," said Martha. Robby looked down at his shoes, thinking how wrong the word "saint" sounded in describing Burke.

The ride home was uneventful. Robby avoided seeing Burke at both the noon and evening meals by carrying his plate up along with the one he took to Miss Stone.

That night as he lay on his pallet, Robby made a plan. Tomorrow he would go to the hospital to work, but first he would follow Burke. Telling his mother that he wanted to get an early start, he would leave before breakfast. He knew the direction the man took. Perhaps he could press himself into a doorway and watch for Burke to walk by. Then he could follow after him and learn where he went.

In the morning, Robby got to the kitchen just before Ma. "I need to go to the hospital today to work for Dr. Bell," he said.

"Take time to eat something first." Ma carried the water bucket to the stove to dip up water for boiling.

Robby shook his head. "I'm not hungry," he said, but he took some bread and a cake of sausage, wrapped the food in a cloth, and put it in his pocket. He hurried down the street, looking behind him every few feet to make sure Burke was not yet out on the sidewalk. Not far from where he had seen the man turn, Robby spotted a house with a sheltered front stoop. He could hunker down there and wait. If someone came out the front door, the worst that could happen would be that they might hit him with something. He had been hit before.

Crouching so that he was not noticeable from the street, he waited. Finally he saw Burke, wearing his stovepipe hat and swinging his walking stick. Robby waited until he passed before he slipped from the stoop and began to follow.

For a time, he moved very slowly, but when Burke turned the corner, Robby ran after him. There were other people on the streets now, and Robby stayed back, his eyes straining for a glimpse of Burke's big hat. Twice he lost sight of him, but both times he rounded a corner to see him again in the distance.

The man walked briskly, a destination clearly in mind. In front of a large tavern, he stopped, adjusted his fancy black jacket, and went inside. Robby was amazed. Was this where Burke spent his days? He had never detected the smell of strong drink on the man.

After a few minutes Robby eased the door open. At first, he could not see into the dark room, but gradually the view became plain. Some men sat at a long bar with a few others at tables scattered about the room. There was no sign of William Burke. Growing braver, Robby stepped just inside for another look. No one seemed to notice him, and he continued to search the room with his eyes. No Burke in sight. Then he saw a door in the back wall. Burke must have gone through that door. Robby backed quickly from the room.

Outside he went to the side of the building. To his delight, a tree grew by a window. He had noticed no window in that side of the tavern. This had to be a window in the backroom. Grasping the lowest branch, Robby swung his legs up to lock around the tree. In no time, he rested comfortably on the second bough, directly beside the open window. Carefully, he stretched his body on the limb, giving himself the perfect view. A strong light came from a lantern inside, and Robby, shaded as he was from the sun, could plainly see William Burke. He sat at a round table with three other men. His top hat and long jacket hung from a nearby rack. His walking stick leaned against the table and the sleeves of his white shirt were rolled an inch or so below his elbows. All of the other men had drinks beside them or in their hands. William Burke had none. All four had wallets, and Robby watched as they removed bills and placed them in the center of the table. Burke rolled a pair of dice. "Come seven or eleven!" he called.

Robby had seen enough. He slipped to the lower branch of the tree, then dropped to the ground. Burke spent his days gambling. Robby knew he should be totally relieved. He supposed many of those same places had a back room to hide gambling, since he had never seen anyone doing it in the taverns where he had often gone to help his father get home. Gambling was probably against the law, but was it worse than robbing a grave? He would need to tell Martha, and he knew he should apologize for being suspicious, but he wasn't sure he could. Besides, what about the name on the walking stick? Martha was keeping secrets from him. Hadn't he told her about Da's cruelty and even about Lolly? Then again, Martha didn't know about the grave robbing. Maybe people were entitled to their secrets.

He took his time walking to the hospital as the thought of what he had seen swam through his mind. It was a nice morning, warmer even than the day before. Spring had definitely come to Philadelphia. On one corner an organ grinder played on his hurdy-gurdy while his monkey held a hat to collect coins. Down the street, a girl sold pretty red and white flowers. When he had earned some money at the medical school, he would buy flowers for his little sister's grave. Then a chill seemed to pass over him. He wondered if he could ever go back to that cemetery where Lolly lay and where he had climbed into graves to steal bodies. He'd best quit worrying about William Burke and his activities. If the Burkes should leave the boardinghouse, Robby would be back to the graves. He would apologize to Martha for speaking rudely to her.

He was surprised to find the thick medical school door locked. He pounded hard against the wood. An older man opened it. "Dr. Bell is expecting me," he said. He was fairly certain that this man was not a doctor. His clothes were those of a laboring man, and he held the handle of a big broom in one hand.

"You the boy Doc said might be coming to help me some?"

Robby nodded. "I am supposed to do some work here."

"Well, I declare! I got me a helper." He extended his hand. "Name's Jenkins," he said, "Jenkins, but you can call me Mr. Jenkins."

"Yes, sir," said Robby, and the man laughed.

"Don't know as I've ever got called 'sir' before. Well, you go tell the doc you're here, then come back, and I'll be most happy to put you to work."

Robby looked down the long hall. "Where would I find Dr. Bell?"

"Oh, he's doing some cutting, showing a group of the young fellows how it's done. That's why the door was locked. Always is when they cut. There's folks might come right in and put up a fuss." He peered closely at Robby. "You've turned right white-faced. Does it bother you, the cutting, I mean?"

"I don't know," Robby said. "It used to, but I saw Dr. Bell repair a little girl's spleen." He bit at his lip. "He couldn't have done that, couldn't have known where the spleen was, without the bodies."

"Well, it gets done around here. Course, they don't get that many stiffs, so when they come in, everybody gets all excited. You'll get used to it if you stay long." He pointed down the hall. "Come on. I'll let the doc know you're here."

Robby followed Lij Jenkins down to the fifth door. "This here is the surgery. All the cutting gets done in here," he said, and he knocked.

"Come in," Dr. Bell called, and Mr. Jenkins stepped inside.

A moment later, Dr. Bell came out with Mr. Jenkins. The doctor extended his hand to Robby, who glanced at it quickly before taking it. There was no blood on the hand. "I'm sorry to disturb you," Robby said.

The doctor smiled. "It's all right. They can finish without me. Tell me, how is your patient?"

"She's stronger, been eating and drinking much better."

"That's good. You come for me if you think I am needed. Now let's see about putting you to work. Lij will direct you. You will earn ten cents for every hour you work. Do you want your pay when you finish each day or after a few times here?"

"After a few times," Robby said.

Dr. Bell turned to Jenkins. "Can you keep a record of the time Robby puts in?"

The man shook his head. "Ah, doc, don't you know I don't do no writing or reading?"

"Sorry, Lij. I forgot. Well, Robby, you do read and write, don't you?"

"Yes, sir."

"I'll trust you to write down your hours for me. There's a big clock at the end of the hall, and there is some paper on that table near the back door. You can leave the paper on the table and write your hours on it each time."

"I will, sir."

"Very well, then. I'll check on my students." The doctor returned to the surgery.

Mr. Jenkins handed Robby the broom he had leaned against the wall. "Here," he said. "You can start by sweeping the hall and the first four rooms. Ain't no classes going on now, 'cept in the surgery. I'll get that later. Dump what you sweep into that can." He pointed down the hall.

Robby liked sweeping the hall and imagining the student doctors who walked there each day, but it was the classrooms he enjoyed most. One had a skeleton hanging from a bar in the front of the room. Robby wanted to study it, but he was afraid Mr. Jenkins or Dr. Bell would come in and see him not working at the assigned task. While he pushed the broom, he stole glances at the bones every time he could. There were also charts in every room like the one he had seen in the surgery, and he did take time to look at one carefully. How did anyone ever know how parts inside the body looked? Of course, the charts had to be created by someone who had cut up bodies.

When he had finished the sweeping, he looked for Mr.

Jenkins. At the end of the hall where he was to write down his time there was a door that led to an area enclosed by a brick wall. Mr. Jenkins was there, emptying a large bucket into a well. "Is that a water well?" Robby asked, and he walked toward the man.

A strong smell came from the bucket, one Robby couldn't identify at first. Jenkins held up his hand to stop him at a distance. "No water here, not anymore. You might not want to come no closer," he said. "I'm getting rid of the parts—you know, the ones left after the doc's done cutting."

Robby's stomach lurched. He knew then that the smell must be of decaying remains. He wanted to put his hand over his mouth and run, but he thought Jenkins might laugh at him. "I'm finished with the sweeping," he said. "I wonder if there is something else that needs doing."

"Be right with you." Jenkins set down the bucket, and Robby could see blood on the rim. Next he picked up another bucket full of a white powdery substance. "This here is lye," he said. "Eats up them parts so we can get more in, keeps down the smell too."

Robby did put his hand over his mouth then, and a gag rose up in his throat. "Go on inside, son. You can have a set down in that chair by the table. I'll come see to you in a minute."

He was glad to have a place to rest his shaky legs, and glad to learn that Lij Jenkins was a kind man. Still, Robby wondered if he would be able to continue working here. Would he ever get used to the smell of decay and the idea of dumping body parts into a well? He looked up to see Jenkins come in the door. "Washed myself up good at the outside pump," the man said when he was near Robby. "Didn't want no smell lingering on me to give you the heaves."

"Thank you." Robby looked down. "I'm sorry I'm such a baby."

Jenkins shook his head and waved his hand in a gesture of dismissal. "Not a bit of it. You ain't no baby. Puked all over myself the first time I saw me a mess of innards. No shame in it, but I tell you, son, you work here long and you'll be proud." He nodded his huge head. "I'm proud to sweep these floors while fellows like Doc Bell is learning them young ones all about making folks well."

Robby liked Lij Jenkins immensely. He was a huge man, even bigger than Da, but he was gentle too. Robby liked how he used the term "son." He could not recall Da ever calling him son. "Help me move some books from room one to room three," Lij said, "then I reckon you'll be done for the day."

When they had finished with the stack of books, Robby wrote down his time. The surgery door was still closed, and he could hear the sound of voices coming from inside. He wanted to go back into the first room to look at the skeleton, but decided he'd better go on home. He knew he had earned fifteen cents, and the idea pleased him.

He had not walked far when Daft Jane stepped from a doorway and stood in front of him. She was clean and smiling, but still wearing her tattered dress. "Jane," he said, "why did you leave the Quakers? They were good to you, weren't they?"

She cocked her head to one side, thinking. She nodded then. "Yes, yes, the Quakers were good. They wanted me to stay, but I couldn't." She looked down at her dress. "They didn't want to give me back my dress, but I wanted it. They washed it, though."

"Oh, Jane." Robby shook his head in sorrow. "Why couldn't you stay?"

"I have to find my baby, but don't fret—they gave me a nice warm blanket, and I've hidden it in my tree. Right near my mother and father."

Robby could think of nothing else to say. He moved to go around her, but she was too quick for him and blocked his way.

Stepping closer, she whispered, "Be careful. They might be watching you."

Even though Robby knew the woman was not rational, a sort of chill passed through him, and he glanced quickly over his shoulder.

"Oh, you'll not see them, but they see you." She nodded her head. "That's for certain."

"I must go," he said, and he made a fast movement to get around her. "I'll have something to give you next time," he called, but he did not look back until he reached the corner. Jane still stood in the street, staring after him.

When he went through the kitchen door, his father was sitting beside the fire, even though the day was not a cold one. "Where you been, boy?" he demanded.

Robby decided to tell him the truth—well, most of it anyway. "I've been sweeping the floor at the medical school," he said, and he looked directly into Da's eyes. "I'll be doing that from time to time, paying for the doctor call and medicine for Miss Stone." He looked at his father's flushed face. "I can work out care for you too, if you're sick."

"I ain't sick, not so much anyway, just a bit bilious and dizzy. I won't have them butchers at that school touching me."

Robby shrugged. He was surprised that his father had not forbidden his working for the doctor. Maybe he was too much under the weather to do so now. Robby drew in a deep breath. He would not let his father stop him. He liked the idea of making money, and he liked to look at the interesting things at the school, except, of course, the body parts.

After the talk with Da, he went upstairs to see Miss Stone and found her sitting in the rocking chair, knitting. "Ah, Robby, how are you?" She put out her hand to take his.

He sat down on her bed and began to tell her about his work at the medical school, about the skeleton, and about the charts on the wall. He did not tell her about what he had been doing when he first saw the chart. "Dr. Bell is going to pay me when I go there to work." He glanced at the door. "I didn't tell Da about the money."

She nodded. "I understand." She pointed toward her bookshelf. "There's a book there on the bottom shelf. See the big black one? Would you get it, please?"

Robby knelt on the floor and pulled the big book from under a stack of others. *"Doctor Bodkin's Complete Guide to Home Treatment of the Human Body,"* he read from the cover. "Oh, this is interesting," he said and he began to turn the pages. "Look," he held up the book slightly, "there's a chart in here like the one at the school."

"I thought you would like it. You can read all about the spleen." She smiled down at him. "You know it would not surprise me should you decide to become a doctor."

Robby sighed. "No, I'm pretty sure it costs a lot to go to the doctors' school, but I'm still glad to get to work there."

She made a sort of *tsk* sound with her tongue. "Don't give up easily on something you want, Robby. That's no way to live."

"Well, maybe." He stood. "Is it all right if I take this with me downstairs?"

"Certainly," she said, "and would you come back for me before supper? I've a mind to go down even if your father is there."

Robby laid six places at the big table while his mother sliced the large meat pie she had made. There were also boiled potatoes, and Robby ate hungrily. William Burke had been smiling when he came into the house. "Things went well at business today," he remarked as he took his place at the table. "My purse is full of money."

Martha shot Robby a quick look, then turned her eyes down to study her plate. "It's glad I am that the day turned out well for one of us," Roger Hare grumbled. "I'm a bit under the weather meself."

Burke dropped his fork, pushed back his chair, and stood. "What are you doing at this table, man? I have no wish to have my Martha around a sick person. In fact, I've no wish to be near you myself."

Robby expected his father to lash back at the man, but without a word Da rose, collected his plate, and went into his bedchamber. Robby's cheeks burned with embarrassment for his father.

Miss Stone looked at William Burke. "I've never seen the man so subdued," she said. "What power have you over him?"

"I am sure I don't know your meaning." Burke's voice was haughty. "I demand what is right, as one who pays dearly for our two rooms in this establishment."

Robby looked at his mother. "Anyone for more hot bread?" she asked.

The rest of the meal passed with few comments. Robby avoided looking at Martha, but after he helped his mother clean the kitchen, he climbed the stairs. He had heard her father go out the front door, doubtless back to his gambling. He needed to tell the girl he had been wrong about her father's work. Her door was open, but he knocked on the frame.

Martha looked up from where she sat at the little table. "Come in, Robby," she said.

He walked into the room and picked up the kitten that came to rub against his legs. "I'm sorry I talked mean to you about your father's work, Martha."

"It's all right. You're the only friend I've ever had." She looked down. "Jacob Taylor was my uncle. Papa brought the walking stick home after my uncle died. He said Uncle Jacob would want him to have it." She raised her head. "Close the door, Robby. I'm going to tell you something about my papa, but you have to promise me you won't tell anyone, not even your mother or Miss Stone."

"You don't have to tell me," he said, but he closed the door.

She shook her head. "I do have to. I'm bursting with need to talk to someone about it." She motioned for him to come closer. "Papa is gone out, but still I don't want to say anything loud." She pointed to the other wooden chair. "Sit close." When he was seated, she leaned toward him. "Do you promise? I mean really, really promise."

"I swear," he said. "Cross my heart and hope to die if I tell."

Martha folded her fingers together, and sat looking down at her hands. The room was quiet for a minute or so, and Robby stroked the kitten in his lap. Then Martha spoke. "In Boston my father worked with my uncle, the husband of my mother's sister. His name was Jacob, like I said, and he was ever so kind to me. My aunt was too. They had no children of their own, but they loved me like I was theirs." She swallowed, drew in a breath, and went on. "One day my uncle fell down a long flight of stairs. His neck was broken." Her lips began to tremble, but she did not stop. "The next day Aunt Susan came to our house. She was crying hysterically, and she told my mother that money was missing from the business. I listened just outside the door, and I heard it all. She said my father took money, and she said she believed he killed my uncle." Martha was crying now, but she went on. "We were already sick, my mother and me, but when Papa came home, he loaded us in the carriage. We left Boston in the dead of night."

"Oh," said Robby. "That's really bad." His head was swimming. Burke had killed his sister-in-law's husband. Robby remembered Burke's cold, dark eyes, remembered the way the man had tripped him, the threat about being able to kill a man with the handle of his stick. Was a killer living right here in Robby's house, eating at every meal with the rest of them, sleeping every night in the room across the hall?

Martha reached out to touch Robby's arm, and his head cleared enough to hear her say, "I think my aunt was wrong, I mean about my papa killing Uncle Jacob. I can believe about the money, but not murder." She shrugged. "But then, it is quite a coincidence, I mean my uncle dying right after Papa took the money. But Papa wouldn't kill anyone. I just can't believe he would do that."

Robby saw that Martha was trembling. He wanted to comfort her. "Lots of people steal. I mean, my Da has taken things from people. He has a new wheelbarrow in the shed right now that he took from someone. That doesn't mean he'd kill a person."

"So you don't believe Papa killed my uncle?"

Robby did believe Burke was a killer. He felt certain of the fact, but he didn't want to say so—not until he had better evidence. "I don't know, Martha, but you don't have to feel ashamed. You aren't responsible for what your papa does. That's what Father Francis says to me about Da."

"Thank you, Robby. Please don't ever tell the police or anyone else."

"I won't. I'm sorry I said that, but I need to tell you what business your papa goes to. I followed him. It looks to me like he spends his time gambling."

"Oh, gambling." She sounded relieved. "He's done that before. In fact, my aunt said he probably had gambling debts to pay, and that's why he . . ." She stopped.

Robby wanted to take her mind off her father. "What's this cat's name?" he asked.

"I've not given her a name, and I must," she said. "I'm sure she doesn't like being called just 'kitten.'"

"Everyone likes to be called by name," Robby agreed. "I hate how Da calls me 'boy' most of the time." He stood up. "Let's go see what Miss Stone says about a name for her."

They found the woman sitting in a chair, her Bible on her lap. "Perhaps you should call her Alley because that is where she came from," she suggested after they told her why they had come.

"Oh," said Martha. "I like that. Alley it is."

Robby went to the window beside Miss Stone's bed. He leaned over to pull back the curtain and look out. It was almost dark, and a terrible feeling of dread came to him. How could he ever go to sleep at night knowing his feeling about William Burke had been right? A shiver went through him, and he tried to think of something else. Daft Jane! He wondered if she had found food. Then he remembered her strange words. They had not disturbed him when she had uttered them, but now with what he had learned about Burke—and now that it was dark outside—Jane's words came back to his mind. He hated to tell Martha that Jane had not stayed with the Quakers. He would put off telling her, but he wanted to talk about what she had said.

"A beggar woman stopped me on the street tonight," he said, still looking out. "I could tell she wasn't right in the head." He stayed facing the window, not wanting to look at Martha, who had settled on the small rug with her cat. "I had nothing to give her."

"Poor thing," said Miss Stone. "Was she angry when you gave her nothing?"

"No," said Robby. "She made a strange remark about someone watching me and said I should be careful." He laughed, but it was a nervous laugh.

"Well, then," said Martha from the floor, "you'd best be careful. My mama used to tell me that sometimes addled people had special gifts. Maybe this woman can tell the future."

"Yes," said Miss Stone, "it is true that sometimes those

who appear weak-minded can have special gifts. I once knew a girl who could add huge sums in her head, but who barely knew her own name. It seems sometimes God gives them special gifts to make up for not giving them common abilities." She smiled. "I doubt fortune-telling is among such gifts."

"So you think no one is watching me?" Robby asked.

"No one watches you, dear. Likely she repeated something she'd heard before, like a parrot." Miss Stone stood up. "I believe it is my bedtime now, so you two should take Alley and run along. I will see you in the morning."

Robby and Martha said their good-nights and moved toward the door. Just before he left, Robby went back to kiss the lady's wrinkled cheek. She put her hand out to touch his face. "You are a dear, dear boy," she said, "and perhaps that woman was, in a way, right about your being watched."

"What do you mean?" he asked.

"Well, she is right about at least one person watching you. I shall watch you always, even when I am in heaven."

CHAPTER SEVEN

Two days later a scream woke Robby. His mother had risen early and gone to help Miss Stone with dressing and preparing for the day, but she had found her in bed, cold and lifeless.

Robby left his pallet and raced up the stairs, knowing what he would find. He stopped at the open door. His mother still stood beside the bed, tears rolling down her cheeks. "She's gone, Robby. Our Miss Stone is no more."

"No!" he cried. "Are you sure?"

"She's cold, son, cold as ice."

"What do we do now?" he asked.

"We'll have to tell your da," she said. "The undertaker must be fetched." She looked about the room. "Her things must be sold to pay for her burial—but then, she did pay her rent early. T'wasn't due until next week, but she give it to me yesterday." Quickly she turned, went to the door, and shut it. "Listen, Robby. I put the money in the kitchen in a jar. Something told me to wait to give it to your da. Let's see if we can keep her death a secret. We'll wait until he's gone out to send for the undertaker. We can use the rent money and let on like the undertaker was paid in advance by Miss Stone."

"Da wouldn't use the money to bury her, would he? Even though her rent wasn't due yet?"

"He would not, and if he got to the body first . . ." Ma stopped and pushed the gray hair from Miss Stone's eyes. "You know what your da would do with her body."

The truth of his mother's words left him weak-legged, and he sank into the rocking chair. "I'll go on down," she said. "There's breakfast to cook. You stay here until you're able to face the others." She went out, closing the door behind her, and Robby listened to her feet on the stairs.

Tears started pushing at his eyes, but he wiped the first ones away. "You can't cry now," he said aloud to himself, "not if you want to save her from being cut up."

He looked around the room and wondered if his father would allow him to keep the books. He would not fight for them, but he would fight if Da found out she was dead and wanted to sell her body. "I know you wanted me to have the books, Miss Stone," he said, as if she could hear him, "and I would be proud to make them mine, but that's not the main thing. The main thing is to see you in a grave. Maybe we can put you beside Lolly."

When the smell of sausage cooking reached the hall and seeped under the door, Robby knew it was time to go down. He had heard Martha and her father already on the stairs. He would need to find a way to get the message to Martha not to go into this room. He pulled the red and blue diamond-patterned quilt his mother had thrown back over the body and, at first, over the face. He changed his mind about that.

For one thing, it did not seem right to cover her so, and besides, if his father should look in for some reason, Miss Stone would appear to be sleeping.

Downstairs Robby stood in the open kitchen doorway, and, unobserved, he looked about the room. His mother moved about cheerfully putting food on the table, and he marveled at her ability to hide her feelings. Then the truth of her life with Da came to him. She had spent years hiding her feelings.

Da sat at the end of the table, and his normal coloring had returned. "Your da feels better now," his mother said as Robby entered the room, "but I told him you were a bit poorly this morning yourself."

His mother was a genius. He smiled weakly. "I am, and I'd not want to spread my illness. I'll just fill a plate for Miss Stone and carry it up to her." He made a bit of an unpleasant face. "I couldn't eat anything myself."

"I've got a plate warming on the stove," Ma said quickly. "Are you sure you don't want me to fill another?"

He shook his head and moved to get the food. William Burke stood in the kitchen doorway. He took out his handkerchief and wiped at his forehead. Robby looked at the white hands and long fingers with well-trimmed nails. What things had those hands done? "I hope the air in this house is not poisoned," Burke said. "It concerns me, one of you sick after the other." Martha stood beside him, and he leaned to look closely into her face. "Of course, my fears are for Martha."

At the end of the table, Da pulled himself up straight in his chair. "Oh, no, no," he said quickly. "Me, I've had bilious spells all me life, and Robby's likely just tired from all the work he done yesterday for the doctors. The boy ain't used to working that hard." He turned his head in Robby's direction. "You come right back down here, and eat yourself a good meal, boy," he said. "You ain't really sick, are you?"

"No, Da, I guess just tired, like you said." He backed quickly from the room.

Upstairs he set the plate on the table just inside Miss Stone's room. He lingered only long enough so that it was believable that a short conversation had taken place, and then he headed back downstairs.

His mother had a filled plate waiting for him. Robby wasn't sure he would be able to stomach a meal, but the breakfast tasted amazingly good to him.

William Burke took his last bite and held his handkerchief to dab at his mouth. "I thought I heard a scream earlier this morning," he said, and Robby could feel the man looking at him. "Surely one of you heard it too."

"It was me," Ma said quickly. "I burned myself with hot water when I washed up this morning. Hope I didn't wake you." She looked down at her plate.

"Hmm," said the man. "It sounded much closer, as if it were upstairs."

"These old houses," said Da, "you can never be sure where a sound comes from. I take to sleep real hard, I do. Didn't hear a thing this morning."

Burke pushed back his chair. "Well, I must be off. Business waits, you know." He kissed Martha on the cheek and was about to walk away when he turned back. "Hare," he said, "doubtless you recall that I mentioned you might want to investigate my business, see if you'd like to take part."

Da was on his feet at once. "I do. I do recall. Would this be a good day for me to join with you, have a look-see?"

Burke looked at Da, his eyes obviously lingering on the man's clothing. "Do you not have any attire more suitable for a gentleman?"

Robby saw his father's face grow red, but he did not appear to be angry. "I've got a coat," he said, "not as fancy as yours, but I've saved it just for special."

"By all means, my good fellow, put it on, and make haste doing so. I will wait in the parlor."

Robby had just finished eating when Da came back from his bedchamber. He had squeezed into a dress coat that Robby could not remember having seen before. It was clearly too small, and Robby followed his father through the swinging doors into the parlor to see Burke's reaction.

Wrinkling his nose in distaste, Burke looked at Hare for only a second. "Well," he said, "if you are to be my associate, we must stop at a clothier for a better coat." He held up his hand in a motion designed to stop any protest. "I'll take the price off next month's rent."

"Yes, yes, of course," said Roger Hare.

"Would you believe it?" said Ma when the men had gone outside. "I don't know what business it is that Burke goes to, but it is something your father wants in on bad."

Robby was about to tell Ma about the gambling, but a thought came to him. "Where's Martha gone off to?" he asked, but the question left his mouth just as the answer came.

A terrified bloody scream split the air, and then came words. "No, oh, no."

Robby ran up the stairs, his mother behind him. Martha

sat beside the bed, her face buried in the quilt. Her body shook with great gulping sobs. Robby put his hand on her shoulder. "There, there, now," he said. "She isn't ailing anymore. She's walking on heaven's streets right now, maybe with Lolly and your mother. Likely, she's telling your mother how glad she was to get to know you." Martha raised her head.

Ma came in then, breathing hard from the quick climb.

"Now, you two listen to me. Miss Stone lived a good life, never harmed a soul. She made the world a better place with her teaching, she did, and she made this household better by teaching you, Robby." She nodded her head decisively. "Her life was good. Now it's up to us to see that she is laid to rest the way she deserves."

She touched Robby's shoulder. "You go to the undertaker's house. You know it, the big white one on Third Street. There's a sign in front. 'Course, I've never read it, but it seems likely it's about the man's business. Tell him to come right quick. Tell him he'll be paid a mite extra if he hurries. Off with you now. Martha and I will take care of things here."

Robby started toward the door, but stopped when his eyes fell on the clothes rack. "Ma," he said, "what dress will you put on her?"

"I was just studying on that myself. I think the yellow one."

"Pa will sell everything else to the secondhand man." He reached out to touch a brown dress with a white collar. "Can I have this one to give to Daft Jane?" He saw Martha glance up. "I mean take it to her at the Quaker House on Sunday."

"Yes, take it," she said, "but don't be dealing with poor Jane or anyone else on the way." She made a shooing motion with her hands. "You can do that later. There's no time for discussion now. We've got to get this dear soul to the undertaker's house afore your da comes home."

Still, Robby grabbed the dress and ran down the stairs and to the front door, where he stopped suddenly. Turning quickly, he dashed into the kitchen, took chunks of bread and sausage, and wrapped them in a cloth. Then he was out the back, the brown dress tucked under his arm with the food inside.

Ma was right about the sign, a big white one with black letters that read BOSTIC AND SON, MORTICIANS. Robby stood in the street looking up at the house. The first floor had lots of windows and a wide door with a cobblestone drive leading to it. Mr. Bostic would need to drive his carriage in and out of the door to deliver bodies and to carry caskets to be buried. A small sign that read KNOCK hung on the door.

Robby squared his shoulders, moved to the door, and did as the sign directed. A boy, a few years older than he, opened the door. "What's your business?"

"We're in need of an undertaker." Robby leaned around the boy to look into the big room. Four wooden shelflike beds jutted out from the walls. Two of those shelves had occupants who were covered with sheets. There was a big table with baskets in the middle, the tips of instruments and brushes sticking out of the top.

"Can you pay? We don't do credit."

Robby nodded. "We can. My ma says that you got to hurry though, and if you do she'll give you extra."

The boy turned toward the stairs at the back of the big room. "Papa," he called. "We got one."

Mr. Bostic came down the back stairs. He was a tall man with a neatly trimmed mustache and a small pointed beard.

"Come in," he called when he saw Robby, "come in and we will talk."

Robby decided to tell the truth. "There's not much time," he said. "One of our boarders died, and Ma wants her to be buried. If my father gets home, he'll say no."

Robby could see that Mr. Bostic was undisturbed by the revelation. He probably had heard lots of strange stories from his customers. "Joseph, quick, bring the carriage round," he called, and the boy disappeared out a side door. "I am Oliver Bostic, at your service. Just let me get my hat and coat." He moved toward a peg in the back of the room, took down a long black jacket and a tall black hat, and put them on.

"Where do you live, my boy?"

"On Sixth Street, number 318. It's in the middle of the block, a big old house with a broken stoop and trim that wants painting."

"Very well, you may ride in our carriage with us. Come, follow me."

It was only a moment before Joseph came around the house with a horse and black carriage. "You can climb in back . . ." Mr. Bostic paused. "I don't believe I know your name, lad."

"Robby Hare." He scrambled up the side to sit in the long carriage bed where he knew coffins often rested.

"Am I to understand that your mother wants the remains taken at once for burial? There will have to be time for the diggers, don't you know?" Mr. Bostic called over his shoulder after the carriage had begun to move down the street.

Robby did not know what to say, but decided Mr. Bostic, who now engaged in a quiet conversation with his son, did not expect an answer.

They were getting close to home when Robby saw Daft Jane sitting on the edge of the street, where she could easily get run over. He wondered if she even realized the danger.

He stood, holding on to the carriage side. "Stop," he yelled. "I need to get out here. I'll run on home and meet you there."

He walked slowly toward the woman, who still sat on the road, using one hand to twist a strand of red hair. "Jane," he said, "I have something for you." He unfolded the dress, unwrapped the bread and sausage he had carried in the folds, and held it out.

She grabbed the food and began sticking large pieces in her mouth. Robby feared she might choke. "Slow down," he said, "you can have it all. There's no rush."

Jane looked at him but continued to chew. Robby laid the dress over one of her shoulders. "Here's a dress for you," he said. "I must go home now." He pulled her up. "You cannot sit in the street so. You're likely to get stepped on by a fast horse. I saw a little girl hurt by a horse just a couple of days ago." He stopped himself from saying it was the child they had seen selling matches. The news would have upset Jane, even though Dolly was healing well.

Jane nodded, but said nothing, just continued her eating frenzy. He pulled at her arm until she stood. He whirled around and began to run. The black carriage sat in front of the house, but Bostic and son had already gone inside. Robby burst through the front door just as his mother had begun to take them upstairs. He noticed a large blanket folded and carried under Mr. Bostic's arm, and he knew immediately how it would be used. He followed them up to Miss Stone's room.

Martha was beside the bed, her face stained with tears.

"Are you a relative?" Mr. Bostic asked. Martha shook her head.

Ma made a *tsk* sound with her tongue. "The dear soul hasn't any family, not one living relative."

"I take it you won't want a funeral, then. Is that correct?"

"No, just a burial, as quick as possible."

"Very well. You should go downstairs now, all of you. We will load the body, then come back inside for payment."

When they were in the hall Ma put one arm around Robby and one around Martha, drawing them to her closely. "We've got to keep her dying a secret," she said. "Maybe we could say a friend come along and took her off to a home in the country, or maybe we could even pretend she's right upstairs all along, until it's too late."

"Too late for what?" Martha asked.

Robby and his mother exchanged worried looks. He had forgotten that Martha did not know about Da's grave robbing. No one spoke for a minute. Finally Ma began to explain. "Mr. Hare likes to dig up bodies, ones just freshly buried. He can sell them to the doctors at the medical schools." A great gasp came from Martha, but Ma went on. "If we don't want her cut up, we must keep her death a secret." Robby shuddered at the thought of keeping another secret.

Just then Mr. Bostic called, "We're coming down now." What had looked like a blanket was actually a bag. Mr. Bostic carried his end down first, with Joseph following.

"Open the door for them, Robby," Ma said. "I'll get the money and the yellow dress."

Robby did as he was told. He opened the door and looked right into Da's eyes. "What in blazes is going on?" Roger Hare, wearing a new suit coat, pushed his son aside and stepped into the hall.

Mr. Bostic was at the foot of the stairs now, his son only a couple of steps behind. "If you will excuse me, my dear sir, I have a body here that needs to be taken to my hearse."

Da reached behind him, slammed the door shut, and shook his head. "Oh, no you don't," he declared, his cheeks inflamed with anger. "I don't know who called you here, but I am the head of this here household. I tell you there will be no body removed from it without me say so."

Mr. Bostic raised his eyebrows, making his dark eyes large. "Am I to understand that you do not wish to see this lady have a Christian burial?"

"Take her back upstairs," demanded Da.

"I think not, my good man," said Bostic. He stepped away from the stair post with his son following. "You may take her back yourself!" They lowered the body, undid the fasteners on the dark bag and slowly rolled Miss Stone onto the floor.

Mr. Bostic handed the bag to his son, who folded it while the father turned back to where Da blocked the door. "Move, please, sir," he said.

Da made no motion. "I will not," he thundered.

"Move, sir," Mr. Bostic said, and his voice was more forceful, and amazingly Roger Hare moved.

"Joseph," Mr. Bostic called over his shoulder, and they both walked out.

"Now, I mean to have the truth of this here trickery. When did this woman die, and why haven't I been told what is happening in me own house?"

Robby could see his mother, who had returned from the

kitchen, getting ready to say something, but he stepped in front of her. "We found her dead this morning, and we didn't want you to know because we were afraid you would do exactly what you are doing right now."

"You bet I am. Likely we need to wait for dark. Not that what we are doing is anyone's business. She has no relations. Still, some people get real worked up over nothing."

Robby pulled himself up straight. "I won't help you, Da," he said. "I can't keep you from doing this, but I won't help you, no matter what you do to me." He braced himself for the slap he expected, and Da drew back his hand.

No one had noticed William Burke come in. He stood in the doorway listening to Robby. "Hare," he said coldly. "Hold your temper. There is certainly no reason to strike the boy. Please step outside with me for a private word." He stepped backward out the door, and Roger Hare followed.

"Come, Martha," Ma said to the girl who cowered in the corner. "Why don't you go up to your room now? You've no need to hear all this business." Then she turned to her son. "Robby, you should go upstairs, bring down Miss Stone's pillow and the quilt from her bed. I won't leave her dumped like a bit of garbage."

When Robby came back down, his mother knelt on the floor beside the body. She took the pillow and put it under Miss Stone's head. Then she spread the quilt over the woman. "We can't stop him, Robby, but we done our best. That's all any soul can do." She had just gotten to her feet when the men came back in the front door.

Burke looked at Robby. "There will be no forcing you to help your father," he said. "I shall be glad to assist him." He turned his eyes back to Da. "I believe Mr. Hare will be . . . what shall I say?" He thought for a moment, then nodded. "Mr. Hare will be less agitated in the future. The two of us are going into business together, and in fact we must go out now." He turned to Ma. "We shall be back shortly for the noontide meal, dear lady."

When they were gone, Ma went to prepare food. Martha, who had not gone up many stairs, came down to go with Robby to the kitchen. Ma gave them potatoes to peel, and she began to slice mutton. "What business do you suppose my husband and your father are going into together?" she asked Martha. "Do you think they mean to rob graves?"

Martha shook her head. "I doubt it. Papa hates to get his hands dirty. My papa is very good to me and he was good to my mother." She sighed. "Robby knows what they are doing."

Robby laid down the potato he had been working on and told his mother about following Mr. Burke.

"Most likely he is using Mr. Hare to help him cheat at cards," said Martha. "I remember that he had a partner like that once in Boston, a fellow to give him hand signals, just little movements of his fingers about the cards. I used to hear them practice. I never told Mama."

Ma nodded. "It's called a skin game, I think. They act like they don't know each other, just go from one game to another cheating people." She shrugged. "Could get theirselves beat up right bad, they could, but I don't think they're likely to end up in jail."

A terrible thought came to Robby. "Ma," he said, "do you think Da or Mr. Burke might have killed Miss Stone in the night, so they could sell the body?"

"Mercy, Robby, your da is not a murderer, nor Martha's father neither, I'd hope. No," said Ma. "If they'd killed her, the men wouldn't have been gone so long this morning. They would have claimed the body at once."

"That's right," said Robby. "I don't know what to do about the doctor's school." He closed his eyes. "I can't stand to think of Miss Stone there on that table. I don't believe I can go back."

"I'd say you must go back." Ma went back to the mutton. "Miss Stone would want you to do it, and Robby, I don't know as she would really mind, I mean being there. You know how she was about folks learning things. She'd most likely want to help the doctors in their studies, don't you suppose she would?"

Robby moved away from the table to wash the potatoes. "She did say I might want to become a doctor, and she was so interested when I told her about the surgery. She had studied the body herself, told me all about the spleen."

"She wouldn't want you to give up your job on her account. You know she wouldn't."

Robby thought about his mother's comment, and they worked for a time without speaking. Finally he said, "I wouldn't say this to Da, but I think you might be right. Miss Stone might not mind at all."

"Well," said Ma, "it's a sure and certain thing the poor dear don't need that old body now." She frowned. "Still, I don't like to think of it. Right now, though, we got to get this meal ready."

Somehow they got through the noon meal. William Burke was concerned because he could see that Martha had been crying. "I'm sad about Miss Stone, Papa. She was so good to me."

"She was old," he said. "The old do not mind dying. They are tired, my pet."

Robby looked down at his plate. He wanted to ask if Jacob had minded dying, but of course, he didn't. How was he going to endure living with the man? Even Burke's voice terrified him. He glanced up at Martha and wished he had made no promises to keep the secret of her father's past safe.

Right after they had eaten, the men went out again, announcing to Ma that they would be taking their evening meal with business associates. Time seemed to drag for Robby, and he was pleased when his mother suggested cleaning Miss Stone's room. "Likely your Da will want to put out the 'Room to Let' sign tomorrow."

They packed her dresses and other clothing in her trunk. Ma gave a pretty little hand mirror to Martha, who had wandered in to watch. "The books are yours, Robby." Ma pursed her mouth, thinking. "Maybe you should keep them in Martha's room for right now. Later when we're sure your da won't raise a stink about selling the lot, we'll take them, shelf and all, to the parlor."

It was a long evening and night for Robby. Long after Ma and Martha had gone to bed, he lay on his kitchen pallet, unable to sleep. The quiet enabled him to hear the town crier shout, "Two o'clock and all's well." It was not long after that he heard Da and Mr. Burke come in. "I'll get the bag and the wheelbarrow from the shed," Da said. "Just give me time to change me clothes. I'd not want to spoil me new duds."

Robby closed his eyes and rolled toward the hearth. His father would need to come through the kitchen to get to his bedchamber. He heard the heavy steps come toward him and stop beside where he lay. Robby pretended to sleep, unable to stand the thought of looking at Da. Then, to Robby's surprise, his father knelt on the floor beside the pallet, and Robby held still while the massive hand rested on his forehead for a minute.

Then Da moved on to his bedchamber. A few minutes later, Robby heard the back door close. He listened for the front door to open, and it did. "There you are," he heard Burke say.

"Let's get the old girl into her bag and give her a ride," Da said.

Robby stuck his fingers in his ears. When he was fairly certain they were gone, Robby lay in the dark thinking. How could Da seem one minute to love him and then be so cruel the next? What strange things must be inside his father. Robby buried his face in his pillow and began to cry. He had not cried like that since Lolly's death. He cried for Miss Stone even now being taken into the surgery. He cried for his mother's hard life. He cried for his father's twisted pain, and he cried for himself and for Martha.

The next morning Da came in early, showing no signs of having been up most of the night. Ma stopped in her breakfast preparation to get him a cup of tea, and he even said, "Thank you, my dear." Robby scrambled up from his pallet, folded it, and put it in the bottom cabinet where his small stack of clothing was kept. He had no wish to be near his father, but he had to add coal to his mother's stove.

Da was in a very good mood, and he couldn't resist sharing news of his good fortune. He leaned back in his chair and announced, "Our Mr. William Burke, why he's a plain genius." Robby paused in the doorway to listen "He's devised an amazing plan with cards. Oh, it's more than a game to him. He's a pure genius, I tell you. Yes sirree, Bob, and I'm proud to be his partner. 'Course, we don't let on that we know each other overmuch. It wouldn't do for other fellows to know we work together. We'll agree on an establishment for cards, and we'll take turns arriving first, never together."

"That's lovely," Ma said, and Robby knew that she meant it would be nice to have her husband out of the house more. It was good news for Robby too. He had decided last night to go back to the medical school, and he did not want to hear his father's comments. He left as soon as the men were gone.

CHAPTER EIGHT

At the hospital, he found the door locked again, and he knocked hard. Jenkins opened the door, dust rag in hand. "Good thing you showed up today. We got lots going on here." He opened the door wide and Robby stepped inside. Jenkins continued, "You can sweep any room 'cept the fifth, the surgery, you know. Doc Bell, he has 'em all closed up, been in there most of the morning." He pointed to the broom leaning against the doorway of room one.

Robby looked down the hall to the door of the surgery. He knew what body lay on that table, and he thought for a minute he might get sick to his stomach. "What's wrong, lad? You ain't looking so good," said Jenkins.

Robby rested against the wall. "I know the woman they are cutting up," he said. "She was a dear lady, who used to be a schoolteacher. She taught me to read and write."

"Makes you feel bad I reckon, but I'd say she might not mind at all, her being big on folks learning." He laughed. "I done told Doc Bell that he can have my worthless carcass when I expire." He laughed again. " 'Course, I expect he would of laid claim to me anyway, living right here like I do."

Robby was glad to have something else to think about. "You live here at the school, Mr. Jenkins?" he asked.

"Sure do; got me a little room with a bed and a wee kitchen." He pointed to the last door on the right. "Don't need nothing else. I used to be the one to get up at night to pay the resurrection men, you know, for the bodies. Lately, though, I ain't been able to hear even when they pound at the door." He pointed to his ear. "Hearing ain't what it used to be. Doc Bell's taken to staying most nights so we don't miss getting in . . ." He stopped. "Sometimes I rattle on too much when I've got someone about to listen to me. I'm sorry about your teacher dying and all."

"Thank you, sir." Robby drew in his breath and reached for the broom.

"No need to call me 'sir.'" He laughed. "Now that we're friends, no need to call me Mr. Jenkins, either, not really. Lij will do just fine." He peered closely at Robby. "Something about you puts me in mind of my son." He shook his head slowly. "Hard to believe he'd be thirty-five now if he'd of lived. He'd be a man, and me likely a grandfather." He did not move away, and Robby sensed he would like to talk.

"How long ago did he die?"

Lij let his breath out in a long exhale. "Oh, near on twenty years. Lost a little girl too, and my wife. Smallpox it was. Took it myself, but I didn't die." He smiled a weak smile. "Wished I had for a long time, sure wished I had."

"I'm sorry, Mr. Jenkins."

"Thank you, son." He put out his hand to pat Robby's

shoulder. "But you call me Lij now." He nodded his head. "You're a good lad to talk to, but reckon we'd best get to work." He moved away, and Robby stepped from against the wall and began to sweep.

Lij called back over his shoulder. "Don't come down around the door today. I'll be doing the emptying, you know."

The door to the fifth room was still closed when Robby went past it to record his two hours on his time sheet. He was glad to leave before the students came out with Miss Stone's blood on their aprons, talking about what they had learned.

Back home, his mother was putting the last touches on supper. He had just washed up to help her when he heard the front door open. Mr. Burke went upstairs, and Da came into the kitchen. He looked glum. "Things went bad, they did." He dropped into his chair. "We lost money, and Burke says it's me fault." He made a sort of groaning sound. "Get me a cup of tea, boy." He rested his face in his hands.

He looked up at Robby as he poured a cup from the tea-kettle his mother had on the stove. "I've got to lay hands on money to make it up to Burke. He's a powerful man, and I ain't desiring to be on the outs with him. The sign should be up about the room. We need to rent it immediately." When Robby set the tea in front of him, he said, "Fetch the sign from the shed, boy, and get the thing up." He shook his head. "Ain't nothing ever done around here without me directing it?"

In the shed, Robby had to move the wheelbarrow to get to the sign. He had made it himself some time ago. It had black letters on a white background. The board he had nailed it to was whittled to a sharp point, making it possible to pound it into the ground. He took a hammer, went to the front of the house, and put up the sign. When he finished, he stood for a moment, looking up. A curtain moved in a window upstairs. William Burke looked down at him. A chill passed through Robby's body, but he made himself wave. The man did not respond. Robby took the hammer back to the shed.

Wanting to postpone another encounter with his father, he walked back to the front of the house to enter. William Burke was no longer at the window, but Robby heard his voice the moment he cracked open the front door. Burke and Da were in the parlor. Robby removed his shoes, eased the door open, and stepped lightly inside.

"I've decided you shouldn't rent the empty room," Burke said. "Not if you want to go into this new venture with me. Take down that sign. We will undoubtedly need it for our activities."

"Well, I don't know." Da sounded distressed. "I never said I'd do it. It's dangerous business. Besides, why couldn't we do our work in your room?"

Burke's voice was cold. "I've no wish to argue with you. Either you are in or out. If you want in, take down the sign."

Afraid he might be caught listening, Robby slipped on his shoes, slammed the front door, and walked to the parlor doorway. "I've got the sign up, Da," he said.

"Take it down," said William Burke. "Your father has decided not to rent the other room at present."

Robby said nothing, but he looked at his father. Da waved his hand to shoo him away. "Do as you are told, boy," he said. Robby went back out to pull up the sign and return it to the shed. What was going on? He was certain William Burke was up to no good, and he was sure his father would follow. His father was a bully, and like most bullies, he was afraid of those meaner than he was.

That evening immediately after supper, the two men went out. They offered no explanation. Robby heard them leave, and stopped stacking dirty dishes at the table. "Do you think they're going to play cards again?" he asked.

Ma poured hot water from the heated kettle into her dishpan, and she shook her head. "No, your da didn't have on his new coat. Even Mr. Burke wasn't dressed up." She sighed deeply. "Don't trouble yourself much about the doings of them two. Thank goodness the good Lord don't hold us accountable for your da's actions."

Later, when darkness came, Robby and Martha read books in the parlor, but Robby found himself going often to the window to look out.

"You're worried, aren't you?" Martha asked.

"I am." He shrugged his shoulders. "I just have a bad feeling, that's all." He thought of telling her what he had overheard, but he decided not to. Martha knew her father was not always honest, but she loved him anyway. No need to make her worry too.

A thought came to him. His father and Burke might be robbing a grave. No, he told himself, it was far too early to go out on such a mission. Still, after Martha had gone up to bed, he took a lantern and headed for the back door. From her bedchamber, his mother called, "Robby, why are you going out?"

He thought for a second, then answered, "I need to check the sign, make sure I put it back in the shed." It was a dark night, perfect for a trip to the cemetery, but Robby was relieved to see the wheelbarrow there in its place, just behind the sign.

He lay awake on his pallet for a long time, listening for the front door. He had propped open the swinging door between the kitchen and the parlor so that he would be sure to hear the men. Sometime after midnight, he fell asleep. He did not wake until he heard them on the steps. "Come on up," said Burke. "We'll have a bit of a drink before we say good night." The voice had a tone more friendly than Robby had ever heard from Burke.

"Sounds fine," said a voice Robby did not recognize. He crept out of bed and through the parlor. He dared not go all the way into the hall, but he could see the first part of the stairs from the entrance.

It was too late. A light came on in Miss Stone's room. He wanted to go up and listen at the door, but he was terrified someone would open the door and discover him.

He decided to go back to his pallet and wait. At first it was easy to stay awake. When he began to be sleepy, he tried sitting up. Finally, when nothing more had happened for a long time, he could fight no longer. He was asleep before he lay down.

His mother woke him with a gentle shake of his shoulder. "Get up," she said, her voice low. "I'm under orders from your da not to make breakfast until Mr. Burke is awake. I'm to wake your da after I hear Mr. Burke stirring about. I'm to feed you, Martha, and myself a cold breakfast in the parlor and then send you out for the morning. Your da woke up just long enough to warn me that there should be no noise in the house, none a'tall."

Ma had already told Martha, who tiptoed down the stairs. They ate bread with butter and thick blackberry jam and drank hot cups of tea. "This jam is so good," Martha whispered.

Ma smiled. "It's my best. I been saving it for special, and I reckon breakfast in the parlor is special." She smiled again, and Robby was struck once more by how hard his mother's life was. He wished he could give her more occasions to smile.

"You two go for a walk or something now," Ma whispered when breakfast was over. "Robby, maybe you'd like to take Martha to Fairmount." Her voice dropped even lower. "I'll get some coins for the omnibus and for something to eat. There's Miss Stone's rent money still in the cabinet. Your da don't know I've got it."

Robby smiled. He loved omnibuses because they sat up high, with a driver even higher. They were more expensive than trolleys, but there were no trolley tracks out to Fairmount Park, two miles outside of the city. Then a thought came to him. They would have to go down to the square to get on an omnibus. They might well see Jane on the streets.

"Martha," he said, "I didn't tell you that I saw Jane a couple of days ago." He looked down for a moment. "The beggar woman I told you and Miss Stone about, that was Jane." He shrugged. "I guess I didn't want you to be disappointed that she didn't stay with the Quakers."

Martha sighed and her shoulders drooped. "Oh, I am sad about that." She pulled herself straight again and then stood. "Well," she said, "I won't give up. Maybe if we keep taking her back, she will finally stay." She looked at Ma. "Do you think we could take her some bread?"

Ma cut two thick slices from the loaf, spread butter and jam on each, then put them together like a sandwich. She wrapped the bread in the dish towel she had spread on a parlor table for their breakfast. "Bring back my cloth," she said. "The poor girl would have no use for it anyway."

"I'll go upstairs ever so quietly and get my big pocket to tie on. We can put the food in there," Martha said.

The day was warm, and buds appeared in the gardens of well-cared-for houses. On one street they saw a small boy running after a goat. "Come back, Lucy," he yelled, and he waved a rope. Both Robby and Martha joined the chase. Robby was surprised at how fast Martha ran, and she was only slightly behind him when Lucy slowed and turned into a garden of a fine home. She helped herself to a bulb that would have soon been a tulip, and she was reaching for another when Robby threw his arms around her neck.

Martha came, laughing, to join them. Just then the back door of the mansion opened, and a women in a white starched apron came charging out with a broom. "Get the beast out of me lady's garden, you little hooligans!" She waved her broom around wildly.

"Please don't hit Lucy," Martha pleaded. "We'll get her out."

The maid continued to swing the broom. She hit Robby slightly with the straw end, but not enough to make him quit laughing.

Together they dragged the protesting Lucy back onto the street to wait for her exhausted owner. "Please don't hit Lucy," Robby mimicked, "just hit old Robby here, instead." They were still laughing when the boy got to them. He thanked them several times, then fastened the rope around the goat's neck and led her away.

" 'Bye, Lucy," Martha called.

The two continued their journey. The brightness of the

day and the thrill of having a little money in his pocket lifted Robby's spirits. Being outside of the house with the broken stoop made him feel free and closer to Martha. "Our fathers are up to something," he said. "Your papa told Da not to rent Miss Stone's room. I overheard them talking about using it for business, and last night when they came in they went up to that room. I think someone was with them, but I fell asleep before they left."

They were in front of a home with a low stone wall, and Martha sank down on it while he spoke. Robby sat beside her, and for a moment she said nothing. Then she began to nod her head. "I think it's still gambling. Yes, that's it. They are setting up their own little gambling house."

Robby didn't agree. "But Da said their plan was dangerous."

"Likely they are laying plans to put lots of money into the game and cheat other men. That could be really dangerous."

"Maybe." Robby frowned. He could not bring himself to tell Martha that he suspected worse. "I'm going to try to stay awake more, see what's going on."

"I'll be watchful too." Martha stood, took Robby's hand, and pulled. "Come on. Let's not let our fathers ruin our splendid day."

Robby could not shake away the dark thoughts. When after a couple more blocks they came to Saint Mary's burial ground, he stopped. "I'd like to walk through the cemetery."

"Why?" Martha asked.

"I'm wondering if there are new graves." They had reached the arched entrance. They stepped inside and looked out over the rows of stones.

"Don't you suppose there are bound to be several new

graves?" said Martha. "That doesn't mean our fathers were digging people up last night. They wouldn't have brought someone home if they were doing that."

"I guess you're right," he said.

"Let's not walk in here." Martha took a step back.

"All right, let's go on down to the square and get our ride to Fairmount. The place is a sight to see. Miss Stone took me there about four years ago. You're going to love it."

Just then he saw a figure hunched against the cemetery rock wall. Martha had turned away, and Robby pulled at her arm. "Wait," he said. "That's Jane." He moved toward the woman, who raised her head. She was wrapped in a shawl that Robby had never seen. He came closer and thought that he saw fear in her eyes. "Jane," he said softly. "I'm Robby." He pointed to Martha who had followed him. "You know my friend Martha too. We would never hurt you."

Jane reached toward Martha. "Oh, your hair," she said. "My little girl had hair like yours." Her shawl fell away from her shoulders, and Robby was glad to see that she wore Miss Stone's brown dress.

Martha put her hand into the big pocket she had tied around her waist and took out the bread. "We've brought you something good to eat."

"Thank you." Jane took the bread and began to take large bites.

Martha sat down on the ground beside Jane. "Do you remember when Robby and I took you to the Quakers' almshouse?"

Jane nodded. "And you held my hand." She stuck the last

piece of bread into her mouth and held out her hand to Martha. "I liked it when you held my hand."

Martha took Jane's hand between both of her own. "Why did you leave the Quakers? You were warm there, and safe."

"I missed my family."

"Where is your family, dear?" Martha asked.

Jane pointed to a group of graves. "Right over there," she said. "My family is over there."

Robby moved to look at the stones. There was a stone for a man and a woman, probably Jane's parents. There was also another stone, smaller, with a tiny angel engraved on it. It read "Beth, daughter of Jane, 1868–1871." Robby sucked in his breath. So poor Daft Jane had really had a daughter, one born the same year he was born, one who had died at three. Robby wondered why no father's name was listed. Was Jane deranged even before the child was born? Likely they would never know. He walked back to where Martha still sat beside the woman on the ground.

"I sleep here, you know," she said as she chewed. "Over there. That willow tree makes a nice little cave, and I have a warm blanket now. Not many people come to the cemetery at night. When it gets colder I'll go with you to the Quakers."

"Martha," Robby said, "maybe we'd better go on our way now. We will come another day and bring you food, Jane."

Jane shook her head several times. "Don't come at night."

"We won't," said Robby.

"You did once, though," said Jane. She twisted her face, thinking. "No, no, that's not right. Robby came twice at night. I saw him. Once I was me and once I was a bird." She smiled.

"I was a great big owl, and I watched what you and that man did."

Robby's face burned with shame. "I shouldn't have done that," he said. "I'll never do it again."

Jane seemed to have forgotten they were there. She began to dig at the earth with her fingernails. "I dream of Jeanie with the light brown hair," she sang.

Robby and Martha walked back through the big gate and out onto the street. At Northwest Square they found an omnibus with FAIRMOUNT painted on it. It looked full, but a boy, slightly older than they, called out to them from the door. "We got room, do you want to come? Won't be another 'bus for an hour."

They climbed the step, and the boy took their money. "Full up now," he yelled up to the driver. "Just squeeze right in," he said to Robby and Martha, "one to each side." Robby sat beside a young man with a large roll of paper between his feet.

"It's drawing paper," the young man said when he saw Robby looking at the roll. "I mean to draw what I see at Fairmount."

Martha sat across from Robby beside a young mother and her little girl. "We're going for a picnic," the child said. "Mama has cheese and bread and some cake." She pointed to the basket on her mother's lap.

Robby leaned back against the seat and looked at the city as it passed. Just outside of town, the bus stopped to let all the passengers out at a park at the foot of a high hill. They climbed out of the bus with the other travelers. "This hill is named Lemon Hill," Robby told Martha He pointed to a big building just below the reservoir. "And see that building? That's where the water for the whole city comes from. They dam up the Schuylkill River and send it out to all the houses. I think that is amazing, all that water traveling around Philadelphia."

"Oh, look," cried Martha, and she ran to a white marble statue in a fountain.

"Miss Stone told me she is called a nymph," Robby said. They watched the water spray up and fall down, and then they wandered on through the park. All of Philadelphia seemed to be enjoying springtime at Fairmount Park. Ladies in brightly colored dresses and big hats walked on the arms of gentleman wearing top hats and coats with long tails. Many of the men carried walking sticks like the one Martha's papa carried, but Robby tried not to dwell on that stick.

They bought two soft pretzels from a vendor and found an empty bench to sit on while they ate. "Yum," said Martha, "these are really good. I've never had one before."

"Pretzels are very popular in Philadelphia." Robby shrugged his shoulders. "I don't know why. They say monks used to make them in Germany or somewhere to give kids who learned their catechisms, and the hard ones got discovered when a baker left some in the oven too long. He just happened to taste one before he threw it away and liked it, so he started making hard ones too."

Two little boys came chasing a hoop that ran directly into Martha. Before the boys could get to her, she stood, handed Robby her pretzel, and sent the hoop rolling. She laughed. "I'd have been mad if that thing had made me drop my pretzel," she said.

When they had finished, they drank from the fountain and bought some chestnuts from a vendor closer to the water.

They settled themselves on a large rock to eat and watch travelers board a big paddleboat powered by steam. "Maybe we'll come back here after I've saved some money from my job and go for a ride down the river."

Martha sighed. "Oh, I hope so, Robby. I hope Papa and I will always stay in Philadelphia. I like living at your house."

"Don't you think you will stay?"

Martha shrugged. "Papa worries me. He doesn't seem happy, the way he was in Boston. Of course, Mama was alive then."

Robby bit at his lower lip. "I'm still worried about what our fathers are up to, Martha. I don't know if it is just gambling." A shudder passed over him. "I have a real bad feeling. Just can't help it."

"I promise I'll tell you if I get any hints about their new business."

They watched two nurses pushing carriages along the walk. "Sometimes I wish I could be a baby again," said Martha. "Babies don't have to worry."

"Well," said Robby, "we'd better start home." He shaded his eyes and looked up at the sun. "It's afternoon now."

On the return trip, the omnibus was not so crowded. Robby and Martha had a seat to themselves. Martha leaned against the window and took a quick nap. Robby did not feel sleepy, but he did not watch from the window as he had on the way there. He closed his eyes and tried not to think about his father and Mr. Burke, tried to pretend he was not afraid of going home to the house with the broken stoop.

Back at the square, men worked at building a sort of platform. Robby and Martha climbed down from the omnibus.

"Can you tell me what it is they are making?" Robby called back to the boy who had collected money for the ride and who was getting off the bus too.

The older boy stepped down to the ground. "You really don't know? Where you been, fellow? Must be a country bumpkin."

"I've been right here in Philadelphia, but I really don't know."

"Why, that's a gallows. There's a man waiting to get himself a nice little swing right here tomorrow. Maybe you'll want to come and watch." He laughed and clapped Robby on the back.

Martha pulled at Robby's sleeve. "Hurry, let's go," she said. "I don't want to watch that thing being built." They said nothing on the way home.

Mr. Burke was in the parlor reading a newspaper. Martha went to put her arm around his shoulder and leaned against him. "Where have you been, my pet?" he asked.

"We went to a wonderful park by the river and ate pretzels. Have you ever had one?"

Burke shook his head. "I have not."

"You must have one. They are scrumptious, and everybody in Philadelphia eats them."

He laughed and reached up to pat her hand. "On your recommendation, I will certainly buy one, my darling."

"And Papa, Robby and I want to go on a boat that travels down the river, but you will need to give me money for that."

Burke frowned. "I don't care for the idea of your sailing on the river with a mere boy." He smiled up at her. "Perhaps one day soon I will take you and young Mr. Hare for such a ride."

Martha clapped her hands. "Oh, that would be lovely, Papa." She looked at Robby. The idea of going anywhere with William Burke made his skin crawl, but he tried to smile for Martha's sake.

Burke folded his newspaper. "I am going up to my bed-chamber now to do a bit of paperwork."

Martha moved toward the stairs also. "I'm going up to see Alley," she said. "She gets lonely when I am gone very long."

Robby could hear his father talking to his mother in the kitchen, and he did not want to go in there. An idea came to him. It would be interesting to see if any changes had been made in Miss Stone's room. He waited until he heard the doors close on both Martha's and her father's rooms. He began to tiptoe up the stairs. Carefully he opened the door, stepped inside, and closed the door behind him.

The room seemed just as it was after he and his mother had cleaned it, except for an unpleasant smell. The trunk holding Miss Stone's things still stood beside one wall, but there was one thing different. The table that once stood by the door had been moved to the center of the room. Three chairs were pulled around it. Burke must have brought a chair from his room. An empty liquor bottle lay on its side, and a half-filled glass stood beside the bottle. There was also a deck of cards.

Maybe Martha was right. Maybe their fathers had brought a gambler home last night. Robby moved to the window at the foot of the bed. Should he open it slightly to air the room? No, he decided to leave it just as he had found it.

He wanted to forget his father and Burke. He would go outside, find something to do where the air was clean. The garden would be a good job. For two days, he worked in the backyard with a shovel turning over soil for the vegetable garden he and Ma would plant. In the shed was a handheld plow left there by his mother's uncle. After he turned the soil, he used the plow to make furrows for planting. For those two days he was tired at night and slept soundly. Still, he was pretty sure that no one came or went from the house.

CHAPTER NINE

On the third night, he woke to the sound of the front door opening. He tiptoed into the parlor, staying close to the wall, and then hid himself behind the big stuffed chair. Someone lit the oil light in the front hall. Robby peeked out from his hiding place and could see three figures Da, Burke, and a woman. Someone made a comment, but Robby could not make out the words. Then he heard a laugh. It was the woman. Robby was surprised to know that a woman would come to play cards with two men. He had not known that women gambled. Robby considered following them upstairs, but returned to his pallet instead. Sneaking around in the dark would only land him in trouble, should Burke or Da discover him. After what felt like hours of tossing and turning, Robby fell asleep. He never heard the woman leave.

The next morning Martha lingered beside him as she moved over to her side of the table. She dropped a tiny piece of paper into Robby's lap, and moved her head ever so slightly, telling him to say nothing. Martha ate little breakfast, only one bite of a sausage. "I'm sorry," she said to Ma. "I seem to have no appetite." She picked up the meat. "If you will excuse me, I'll just take this up to Alley." She kissed her father's cheek and left the room.

Robby wanted to leave the table too, but he knew that might arouse suspicion. He ate a big sausage and some buttered bread. Burke lingered over his breakfast for what seemed like forever. When finally the man was out the front door, Robby went into the parlor. Even though neither Da nor Ma could read, he did not want to be questioned about the piece of paper. The letters were small, but Robby's eyes were good. "Come to my room when you can. I've something to show you."

He walked back to the swinging door, opened it slightly, and said, "Ma, I'll be back in just a minute to help clean up. That kitten is loose. I saw it on the top stair."

"I won't have the thing down here," said Da, but Robby did not wait to reply. He bounded up the stairs two at a time and knocked lightly on Martha's door.

She let him in at once. In her hand was a woman's shoe. When the door was closed, she handed it to Robby, then sank to sit on the edge of her bed. "I stumbled over it in the hall last night. Something woke me. Maybe it was the closing of the front door. I decided to see if Papa was in his room. He wasn't, but I found that lady's shoe. Is it your mother's?"

Robby studied the shoe, a well-worn lady's black slipper with a pointed toe. He shook his head. "It's not Ma's or Miss Stone's."

"How do you suppose it came to be in the hall?"

Still holding the shoe, he moved about the room, trying to decide what to say.

"Robby," Martha said, "tell me what you are thinking."

"They brought a woman home with them last night. I

heard them come in, and I heard her laugh." He pulled a chair from the table, moving it so that he could see Martha's face. "I never heard anyone leave."

"But why would she leave a shoe behind?"

He shrugged. "I don't know, except maybe if she got really drunk. I know they had strong drink in that room before. Maybe they got her drunk so's to be able to cheat her out of money. Maybe she was too far gone to notice when her shoe fell off."

"Is that what you think?"

He shrugged again. "I don't know, Martha. I just don't know what to make of the shoe. What would your papa do if you asked him about it?"

"I don't like to think of questioning him." She closed her eyes for an instant. "But why do I hesitate? Papa has never been unkind to me. I don't believe he ever would be."

"Think about it." He stood. "I've got to go help Ma, and then I am going to the medical school to work." He walked to the door. "I'll see you later."

At the school, he found the door unlocked. "Doc ain't here," Lij Jenkins said. "He had to go check on his mother, her living alone and all. Number five's all locked up. He's got a stiff in there waiting. There's classes in all the other rooms." He looked down. "The hall can stand sweeping, though." Robby got the broom, and while he worked he thought. Finally, he faced the notion that had played about the edges of his mind since he saw the shoe: maybe the woman did not leave the house alive.

A great shudder passed over him. What if Da and Mr. Burke had killed the woman last night! He felt weak and sick. He gave himself a shake. No, he wouldn't let himself think of such a thing. Murder could not have happened in his very own home.

Students came out of room three and walked past him. They talked and joked among themselves, but Robby heard nothing. For a time he could not move, frozen with fear. Finally, he forced himself toward room three. He needed to sweep that room. He took his broom and went in.

At the front of the room, a white cloth covered a table. He lifted the edge to see what was covered. Two eyeballs and a tongue lay on a tray. Robby thought they must have only recently been removed. Once the thought might have sickened him, but now that he had begun to suspect murder in his own home, nothing small like body parts could bother him. He studied the tray's contents until Lij stuck his head into the room. "There you be," he said. "Thought you done gone, but I couldn't find my broom."

He walked into the room to stand by Robby. "Interesting what you find around here, ain't it." He looked closely at Robby. "You all right, son?" He took the cloth from Robby and spread it back over the table.

At first no words would come from Robby's throat. Then he said, "I'm all right, Lij, but things may not be at my house. I've got to go home." He reached for the broom and handed it to Lij. "I've got to go home," he repeated. "Got to write down my time and go home. Ma will worry if I'm not there for the noontide meal."

He did not hurry home, however. Rather he walked slowly, his mind whirling with thoughts and images. There was the shoe. Would Martha ask her father about it? When finally he did reach home, he went in through the back door.

Ma was in the kitchen. "Noon meal is over," she told him. "Your da's been drinking already, sleeping it off. Mr. Burke is here, come in unexpected to eat. Good thing I had plenty. I saved a bowl of stew for you. There on the back of the stove."

He shook his head. "Not now, maybe after a bit." He wandered into the parlor and stood listening. The house was quiet. He wanted to go up to see Martha, but he felt certain her father would see or hear him. Just then, Burke appeared, coming down the stairs. "There you are, my boy. I've been waiting to talk with you." His words were pleasant enough, but his voice and eyes were even colder than usual.

Robby swallowed hard, trying to think what he might say, but Burke gave him no chance to speak. "Be so good as to follow me outside, please," he said, and without looking back, he opened the front door and went out.

"Don't shake," Robby told himself. "Don't let him see you're afraid." He went out, and Burke, standing on the stoop, pulled the door closed. Because of the broken board, there was no room for Robby on the stoop, so he stepped down and turned in Burke's direction.

"Martha found a shoe," Burke said. "Undoubtedly she told you. I explained to her that your father and I had a couple in last night to play cards. The woman, Margaret was her name, grew quite intoxicated, and had to be helped down the stairs by her husband. Obviously her shoe fell off without their realizing it." He cocked one eyebrow and leaned toward Robby. "Do you understand me, my boy?"

Robby nodded his head. "Yes, sir, I do."

Burke opened his jacket, and Robby saw a leather scabbard fastened by a strap that ran over his shoulder. Burke pulled a long knife from the holder. He held it out, carefully moving one finger down the side that was not sharp. "That's good, good that you understand. Have I showed you my knife, I wonder?" He did not wait for an answer. "I always keep it razor sharp. It could slice right through a throat—for instance, your mother's."

A gasp escaped from Robby. "Ah, I see the thought troubles you. She is a hardworking woman and a good cook." He paused for a moment. "Of course, she is rather common, but still one should hate to see anything happen to her." He stepped down to stand almost nose to nose with Robby. "Keeping your mother safe is simple, my boy. Stay out of my affairs. Oh, and of course, you will not mention this conversation to my daughter. Martha has had a good deal of heartbreak in her life already. I forbid you to add to her pain, and I would know, Robby. Believe me, I would know, even if she said nothing to me." He nodded his head. "I know my daughter, know her very well, and I can read her reactions easily. Let her forget the shoe, and never mention this conversation." Without another word, Burke put back the knife, picked up the walking stick he had leaned against the door, and strode away, whistling.

When the man was out of sight, Robby ran to the back of the house where the shed stood, door closed. He yanked it open. When he had put away the plow, he had put the sign in front of the wheelbarrow. Now the sign was behind. The wheelbarrow had been taken out the night before. Da and Burke had taken a body to the school last night. Robby remembered the laugh he had heard as he lay on his pallet. They must have killed her upstairs and sold her body to the school.

He began to shake uncontrollably. He stared at the house,

the house that sheltered two men who had murdered a woman last night, a woman whose shoe he had held in his hand. And the night before! Someone had come home with them then too. Two people had undoubtedly been killed. How had they done it? Somehow he felt sure Burke had used his hands, those awful pale hands with the long fingers. He could not go back inside the house, could not face his father. Nor did he want to see Martha or Ma. What would he say to them? Should he tell them the truth? He could not even make himself go in to tell Ma he was leaving. Continuing past the house with the broken stoop, Robby walked for hours without aim, but then he made a decision. He had to go to the medical school, had to know for sure. Still he did not hurry. He moved slowly, as if half asleep.

In Northwest Square, the gallows was completely finished. It stood out against the sun. Nearby, a group of girls, totally unconcerned about the upcoming execution, jumped rope. They chanted, "Cinderella dressed in yellow went upstairs to kiss her fellow." They laughed, and Robby watched with envy.

The tallest girl looked over her shoulder to speak to him. "Do you want a turn?"

He shook his head. "I've got to go on," he said, and, head down, he moved away.

The door of the medical college was locked, and he pounded hard. Lij came to let him in. The hallway was dark after the bright sun, and Robby could not see the man's face. "I had to come back," Robby said. "Had to see Dr. Bell."

"Something you need?" Lij asked.

"I've got to ask Dr. Bell something."

Lij pointed down the hall. "He's in the surgery. You want me to see if he can come out?"

"No," said Robby, "I'll wait." Lij disappeared, and Robby stayed near the door until he could see, then began to move down the hall. Rooms one, two, three, and four were empty. At the door of room five, he stood still and listened for a while. He could hear voices, but not what was being said. Robby paced up and down the hall. Maybe it was a man who was being cut up. Maybe he had gotten himself worked up over nothing. Then he would close his eyes and see Burke's hands around a neck. Finally, he could wait no longer. He took the knob, turned it, and pushed the door open slowly. A large group of young men were gathered about the table.

Robby could not see the body, nor did he spot Dr. Bell. The room was flooded with light, and filled with the smell of blood. He wanted to run, run outside and vomit, but he made himself stand still. He could feel eyes upon him, and he wished he had not come.

Dr. Bell stepped out from the group. He had a knife in his hand. "What is it, Robby? Do you need me?"

Robby could not speak, but he nodded his head. The doctor handed the knife to one of the students. "Go ahead, Farley. You may take out the heart." Dr. Bell walked to a basin, poured water from a large steel pitcher, and washed his hands.

Next he came to Robby, put his arm around him, and led him from the room. "Something is wrong. Tell me, Robby," he said when they were in the hall.

"Did someone bring in that body last night?"

The doctor nodded his head. "That's right."

"I couldn't see it, not well." Robby swallowed hard. "Is it a woman?"

"Yes."

"My da? It was him who brought her in, wasn't it?"

With his arm still around Robby, Dr. Bell began to move. "Come to my office. I think we need to talk." The doctor opened a door on the left side of the hall. Robby had never seen the office. A big desk made of dark wood stood in front of a large window. Bookshelves lined the walls, all of them full. There were also books stacked in corners. Three chairs sat in front of the desk, and Dr. Bell pointed to one. "Sit down, please." The doctor walked behind the desk and took that chair. "We take a vow not to tell who brings us the bodies. It's the only way our arrangement works. Still, I am aware that you were with your father when he brought the first to me."

"I was," Robby said, almost in a whisper.

"I remember. I knew you were an unusually bright boy even then, and I knew you hated what your father was doing."

Robby nodded. "I did."

"It is a despicable thing, digging up a body after a broken-hearted family has buried it." The doctor leaned back in his chair. "I understand why it troubles you to have your father involved in such work. I wish there were another way to get bodies, but there isn't. Think about this, Robby. Lives will be saved because of what those students are learning today from the body brought in last night, lives like little Dolly, who will be strong enough to leave the hospital soon."

Robby bit at his lip. He wanted to tell the doctor that his father had murdered the woman, but he knew he couldn't. They would come and take Da away and Mr. Burke with him.

Martha would be heartbroken, and Ma. He could never forgive himself if Burke hurt his mother.

The doctor pointed at one of the two portraits that hung on the wall behind Robby's chair. "That's Benjamin Franklin," he said. "You know who he was, don't you?"

Robby turned in his seat to see. "I've read about him, and I've many times seen the statue. I've seen his grave too."

"Well, Franklin and the other man, Dr. Thomas Bond, founded this hospital and later this school. We had the first hospital in America and the first medical school, right here in Philadelphia. That was almost one hundred years ago, Robby, but we have so much more to learn about what is inside human beings, so much more. We cut people up in an effort to save lives."

Robby wanted to stand up. He had to get away from Dr. Bell before the truth came pouring from him. He was not certain he could get up, but he did. "I need to go home now." He started toward the door, but turned back when the doctor spoke.

"Did you know this woman, Robby?" The doctor's eyes were kind.

Tears came up from inside him, but he held them back. "Just a little bit," he said. "She had a nice laugh." He went out then and hurried to leave the building.

There was nothing to do now but go home. Ma would need him to carry in the bucket of coal from the wagon that drove down the street just before supper. Girls still jumped rope in the square. Robby wondered if they had been at the jumping since he had come earlier, but he did not say anything. The tallest girl smiled at him, but this time she did not ask him to join. Their chant was different now. "Benjamin

Franklin went to France to teach the ladies how to dance. First the heel, and then the toe, spin around and out you go."

Robby thought that every child of any age in Philadelphia knew who Benjamin Franklin was, but they probably didn't know that he started the first hospital in America, and they probably did not have fathers who murdered people to sell to the school in that hospital.

At home he found Da in the kitchen. He sat at the table, a large bottle of liquor in front of him. There was no glass, and as Robby watched, Da tipped up the bottle for a big gulp. "Come sit down, me boy," he said when he finished, and he pointed to the bench beside him.

"I don't want to sit down, Da."

His father bowed his huge head. "Oh, I'd not blame you for that, Robby, not one little bit. I've done things I can't speak of, terrible things. Things that will send me to hell for certain, but I can't confess to a priest."

Robby's mother came in then. She carried a bucket of coal, and Robby rushed to take it from her. "I'm sorry, Ma," he said. "I should have been here to do that for you."

"A body might think the man of the house could do such." She used her head to point toward Roger. " 'Course that one couldn't get his own self in from the coal wagon, let alone carry a bucket."

Robby put the coal into the great stove, then turned to his mother without even trying to keep Da from hearing his words. "Let's leave him. Let's get out of this miserable house."

"Go on." Da waved his hand toward the door. "I'd feel better, feel better about the both of you, was you to leave. You'd be safe then."

"Safe? Safe from what?" Ma demanded, but Da had collapsed facedown on the table. "Come help me, Robby, we got to get him to his bed."

Robby bent to put one of Da's arms around his shoulder, and Ma took the other arm.

"Wake up, Roger," Ma urged, but Da kept his eyes closed. They stumbled into his bedchamber. As soon as his father was deposited on the bed, Robby escaped out the back door.

For several hours, Robby worked in the backyard, taking a hoe and tracing the rows he had plowed. It was a totally unnecessary job, but it gave him something to do, some reason to be out of the house. He wanted to leave, but he was afraid that Burke, when he came home for supper, would think his absence a sign that he had gone to the police. He would have to eat with the man, have to sit at that table and act normally.

At dusk, Robby went inside. The evening meal was almost ready, his mother pulling a pan of baked cod from the oven. "Is Mr. Burke here?" he asked.

"He is." Ma set the pan on top of the stove and began to fill plates. "Run up and tell them supper is ready." But before he could move to the swinging door, Burke and Martha came in.

"Something smells delicious," Burke said, and he smiled. "We are starved, aren't we, darling?"

"Yes," said Martha. "I should say so."

Robby searched her face and was amazed to see no sign of distress. She believed what her father had told her about the shoe. If Robby told her the truth, she wouldn't be able to hide that knowledge from her father. A picture of Burke's knife flashed through his mind. He took his place on the bench.

"Where is our Mr. Hare?" Burke asked. "He will be eating with us, will he not?"

"Roger don't feel so good," said Ma. "I'm afraid he's had way too much of the drink."

Burke made a *tsk* sound. "What a pity. Strong drink can become such a vulgar, unsightly habit. 'Tis why I never touch it."

"I'm going out," Robby said to Ma when he was finished. "I won't be back till bedtime. Don't worry about me." He hurried to the back door, but his mother followed him outside.

"Not coming back till bedtime? For mercy's sake, Robby, what will you be doing all that time?"

Robby shrugged his shoulders. "Don't know. Likely mostly walking. I'm too restless to sit about."

His mother reached out to lay her hand on his cheek. "Ah, Robby, you're such a good boy, and me with no way to make your life better." He gave her a quick hug and moved down the alley.

For a long time, he walked tree-lined streets and listened to the peeping chorus of tree frogs. It was a friendly sound, and he wished he could crawl up into a tree and become part of it. Folks called Philadelphia the city of brotherly love because William Penn, who founded Pennsylvania, was a Quaker and wanted religious freedom for everyone. He walked with head down, feeling no love except maybe in the call of the frogs.

On Locust Street, he stood for a time and watched ladies and gentleman going into the opera house. A big sign read WAGNER'S THE FLYING DUTCHMAN. One lady in a soft blue dress stopped and looked at Robby. She reached into her small handbag and took out several coins. "Here, child," she said, and she extended her gloved hand toward Robby. "Take these, and God bless you."

Robby stepped backward. "No, thank you, ma'am," he said softly. "I'm not a beggar." He whirled about and ran. When his legs grew tired, he headed home, glad to be exhausted. Surely he could sleep tonight. Tomorrow he would think. He would think until he had decided what to do about Da and Burke.

Ma sat dozing in the kitchen rocking chair, and he touched her arm. "You shouldn't have stayed up, waiting for me," he told her. "Is Da asleep?"

"Out with Mr. Burke." She yawned. "I'm going to bed. Good night, my Robby."

"Don't think about Da and Burke," he told himself. He spread his pallet and fell into blessed sleep. In the wee hours of morning, he woke when Martha's cold hand covered his mouth. "Ssssh," she whispered. "I've got to talk to you, but I'm afraid someone will hear us."

Robby sat up, rubbing his eyes. "Are they back yet? Our fathers, I mean."

"They're back and in their beds."

Robby looked quickly toward the door to his parents' bed-chamber. Enough moonlight came in through the window to allow him to see that it was closed. Still, they must be very quiet. There was nowhere else to talk. In the parlor or up in Martha's room, Burke might overhear them. It was safer to take the risk of Da's hearing. He rose, took Martha's hand, and led her to the far corner. "We've still got to whisper," he told her.

"I've been thinking about what you said, you know, about being afraid our fathers were doing something worse than gambling. When Papa came into my room tonight to say good night, I got this awful feeling, and I decided I wanted to know the truth. I didn't go to sleep. At first I sat up and read, but it was hard to concentrate on a story. Finally I just turned out the light and got in bed to wait, listening for them to come in the front door."

She drew in a deep breath and squeezed Robby's hand. "I could tell someone was with them on the stairs. After they went into Miss Stone's room and closed the door, I tiptoed across the hall to see what I could hear. Sure enough, they had a man with them."

"What were they doing?" Robby had begun to shake; not wanting her to know, he turned Martha's hand loose.

"For a long time they played cards and drank, our fathers urging drink on the other man, called Lewis. I was just about to give up and go to bed, when finally your father says, 'It's late, my friends. Lewis, why don't you just stretch out on that bed and get yourself a bit of sleep?'

"I hurried back to my room then, but I peeked through a crack in my door. The room got totally dark, and our fathers came out, but they didn't go very far. Your father just stayed in the hall. Papa went to his room, and came back with a white pillow that I could see in the dark. They waited for a while, listening, and then they went back inside. I was scared, almost to death. I wanted to run and get you, but I was afraid they would come out and catch us."

"What happened next?"

Martha bowed her head, and for a minute she said nothing. "Martha," Robby said again, "what happened?"

"I crept back to the door to listen. At first, I couldn't hear anything. Then there was a good deal of noise, like someone thrashing about. Then I heard my papa say to your father, 'Hare, get yourself over here to hold him down.' I got too scared then and ran back to my room. I heard them leave, just the two of them, not the man named Lewis. As soon as I was sure they were asleep, I slipped down here to tell you." She started to cry. "What do you think happened, Robby?" she asked between sobs.

He sucked in his breath. "Martha, you know what happened. It's awful, but we've got to face the truth. Our fathers killed a man tonight."

"Oh, Robby, I think the same thing." She reached for his hands. "I hate to think it, but I am afraid Papa must have put that pillow over his face. Oh, Robby, my papa must have killed a man with the same pillow he's sleeping on this very minute."

"Did you hear anything else?"

Martha tried to stop crying, but she couldn't. "I heard Papa say they'd have to leave him a couple of days, something about the doctors getting suspicious if they take another one in so fresh. I couldn't just lie there by myself. I had to come tell you. What do you think they meant, you know, about being too fresh?"

For a second or two no one spoke. Martha reached out to touch Robby's shoulder. "Robby, what did they mean?"

"Your papa said they couldn't take another fresh body to the school. That's because they killed the woman who wore that slipper and sold her last night." He drew in another deep breath. "And there was a man before that. I'm pretty sure they killed him too. I think they must bring home people who are all alone, you know, street people who don't have anyone to look for them." He paused for a minute, then went on. "Your papa threatened me with his knife earlier today, showed me the blade, and said he would slice Ma's throat if I meddled in his business."

Martha gasped. "What are we going to do?"

"We have to go to the police," he said.

"But they will hang them. They'll hang our fathers, Robby." She covered her face with her hands. "No, please don't go to the police."

"We can't let them keep bringing home people to murder. We just can't."

Martha sniffed back a sob. "I know. I know, but they won't bring home another one soon, not with Lewis on the bed. Maybe we can think of some other way to stop them. Will you wait, just a little while, please?"

"Martha, listen to me. We cannot wait long, and if your papa has any reason to think you know, he will kill Ma and me."

"I won't let on, but promise you won't go to the police tomorrow."

"All right," he said. She went back upstairs, and he lay in the dark, thinking, until daylight came into the house with the broken step. The next morning he told his mother, even though he had not planned to do so.

"Get up, Robby," she said when she came into the kitchen. "No wonder you're tired. Seems like nobody in this house was sleeping last night. Noises kept waking me up."

"Burke and Da killed a man last night. Killed him in this house and his body is upstairs in Miss Stone's room."

His mother gasped, and for a long time she held her breath.

Robby's eyes went from his mother to his father, who had just come from his bedchamber.

Ma saw Da too, and she whirled toward him. Her face turned white, and she grasped the edge of the table as if she thought she might fall. "Is it true, Roger?" she asked. Da said nothing, but he dropped into his chair, his face in his hands. "Roger." Ma's voice was louder this time. "Answer me. I mean to know the truth."

Da put his finger to his lips. "Ssssh, don't let Burke hear you," he whispered. "It's him that is the killer, and he'd kill any one of us just that quick."

Ma sank to the bench. "Roger Hare, you'll hang same as him, and that's a fact."

Da put his finger to his lips again. "Not if you two keep quiet. The man's planning to leave Philly soon. We've got to keep quiet till he's out of this house." He put his hands out flat on the table and studied them for a minute before he spoke again. "Them three we did wouldn't have lived long anyway. Surviving on the street the way they did, bound to be ate up with disease." He stood. "Get yourself together, both of you, and put breakfast on to cook."

CHAPTER TEN

Somehow they got through the morning meal. Ma even talked to Mr. Burke about the weather. "Awful cloudy outside this morning," she said. "I expect we'll have a rain before the day's over."

Burke stood. "I'd best get to my business before it starts, then." He leaned to kiss Martha on the head. "Why not take a nap, darling? You look tired. Not sick, are you?"

It surprised Robby that Martha could smile at her father, but she did, smiled up at him sweetly. "Maybe a bit of a cold. I believe I will go back to bed." She stood too.

Da waited until the Burkes were gone, and then he too left the table. "Mum's the word," he said. "They'll be gone soon, and we can go back to living decent."

The rain started before Robby and Ma had the kitchen cleaned. Robby opened the back door and stood staring out. "Don't think about anything bad," Ma whispered to him, and then she took the last plate from the table. "Just don't let yourself think, son." Robby saw that her hands shook so that it was hard for her to hold the dish. "Promise me you won't say nothing?" Tears filled her eyes.

For a long moment Robby could not speak. "Robby?" His mother set the plate she held back down on the table. "Robby, promise me."

He closed his eyes. "I promise, Ma," he said. "At least for now."

Ma stepped around him to pull the door closed. "Too much dampness in your lungs is likely to make you sick."

"I am sick already, Ma," he said, "sick nearly to death." He went to the parlor and from there into the hall, where he stood staring up at the stairs. Why did he want to go up there? Surely not to see the dead body.

It was as if something pulled him. By the time he had reached the landing, he had broken out in a sweat. From the top of the stairs, he saw a big iron padlock. Burke had made certain that the door would not be opened. There were two chains also, one nailed to the door and one to the door frame, with the lock between them. Robby let out a long breath, relieved that he could not go inside. Still, a thought came to his mind.

When it had stopped raining, he went outside onto the new, wet grass. Looking up, he could see the window to Miss Stone's room. "Don't think about it," he told himself aloud. "You can't get up there." Even so, he walked to the tree that grew beside the house.

He could climb that tree. He *had* climbed that tree, summer before last. He was taller now. From the tree he could reach a ledge that ran along at the top of the first story. From that ledge, he could pull himself up to the open window of Miss Stone's room.

"But why?" Again he spoke aloud, but even before the last word was out of his mouth he was climbing, climbing fast. He did not slow down until he pulled himself up by the window ledge. Then he froze. A man lay dead on the bed directly in front of the open window. Robby could have reached out his hand to touch his face, but, of course, he did not. The head was turned in his direction, and the mouth gaped wide, showing rotten teeth, and the eyes, his terrible open eyes, stared out at Robby. He began to tremble, and he feared he might fall.

Lowering himself slowly, he searched with his foot for the ledge. It seemed a long time before he found it. Next he grasped the tree, his arms wrapped around the large branch. Now he slid quickly, unaware that the bark bit at his skin, tearing his shirt and making him bleed.

When his feet touched the ground, he sank down and sat hunched over, his arms hugging his raised knees. Still breathing heavily, he rested for only a moment. Then he got up and began to run. Maybe he would run away, and never look back. After a few blocks, though, he slowed. Where could he go? Besides, there was Martha and Ma to consider. There was always Ma.

It surprised him to see that he stood in front of St. Mary's Church. Maybe he could go inside to sit still and think. Candles burned in the dark church, and Robby's heart stopped racing as soon as he stepped inside. He stood for a moment, drawing in the smell of the candles and of the polish used on the altar. He slipped, then, into a pew at the back, leaned on the seat in front, and rested his head against his arms there.

It was only a few minutes before a voice said, "May I help you, my son?" Robby looked up to see Father Francis. "Robby? Is that you, Robby Hare? We've not seen any of your family at St. Mary's for a long time."

Robby nodded, but he said nothing. "Is something troubling you, Robby?"

He wanted to tell everything. Weren't priests bound to keep your secrets? He bit at his lip, maybe not when those secrets involved murder.

He drew in a big breath. "Father Francis," he said. "Does a person always have to keep a promise?"

"When we give our word, we should honor that promise."

"Even if people might get hurt?"

"Well," said the priest, "we cannot allow someone to harm others just because of a promise. Do you want to tell me what troubles you?"

Suddenly Robby was afraid. What if Father Francis got concerned about him? What if the priest came to the house with the broken stoop to ask questions? Burke wouldn't hesitate to kill a priest. Robby was certain of that. His mind raced. "A boy I know, his name is William. He made me promise not to tell that he's been stealing his father's liquor."

It was too dark to be sure, but Robby thought the priest smiled. "Likely William's parents will discover what the boy is up to. I'd say let those in charge of the boy deal with him."

Robby nodded his head. "Thank you, Father. I feel better." He stood up.

"Tell your mother and father I asked about them."

"I will," he said, and he left the church. He would go home and wait. Father Francis had said to let those in charge handle the problem. Robby would wait for just a time, but he would not, he promised himself, let another person die.

Da stayed drunk most of the next two days, not appearing for meals. Mr. Burke still dressed himself up every day, leaving right after breakfast with a kiss for Martha. "I'm off to business," he would say. Robby supposed his father had not proven very good at cheating at cards, because Da was never invited again to join Mr. Burke.

Somehow Robby got through the days. He read with Martha, helped his mother in the kitchen, even ate at the table with William Burke, and worked extra hours at the medical school. All the time, his mind felt frozen and his body seemed to move through a great fog.

In addition to sweeping out the classrooms, he began carrying out buckets of body parts to dump in the well. The work no longer made him sick to his stomach. Numbness made him unable to feel anything.

He managed to stay away from Dr. Bell, afraid the doctor might see something in his eyes, might guess his torment. Robby knew if he talked long to the kind man, he would blurt out the truth.

Lij Jenkins saw a change in him. "Something eating at you, Robby?" he asked one day.

"I can't talk about it, Lij," he said. "I got problems at home. My da's an awful drunk."

"Does he hurt you?" The anger in Lij's voice touched Robby.

"He used to, but not anymore." It was true. Da had not hit him or Ma now for a long time. Robby would give anything to go back to those old days when all he had to worry about was Da's slaps.

"If ever you want to get away, you come here. You hear me? I know where there's an extra cot we can put in my room."

"Thank you, Lij." Robby moved on down the hall.

During the night, he planned, lying awake for long hours. Sometimes he told himself he would go to the police in the morning. At other times he would plan to kill William Burke. He could take the hatchet from the shed, creep upstairs, and smash the man's head in. Could he really do that? If he did, would he be hanged for the crime?

On the second night, he heard the two men carry down the body. Lewis, whose terrible face came over and over to Robby's mind, was about to make his last journey, a journey that would end at the medical school. Robby decided he would go to the police in the morning, and he did, leaving before anyone was awake.

He knew his way about town, and it was not a long trip to Chestnut Street, where City Hall, a two-story building made of red brick, seemed small between its two neighbors, the Philadelphia County Courthouse and Independence Hall. Robby knew the police station was on the first floor of City Hall. He walked to the door, pulled it open, and turned to run. What if William Burke had become suspicious when Robby failed to show up for breakfast? What would his mother say if Burke questioned her? At this very moment Burke could have his terrible knife at Ma's throat.

When he burst through the back door, Ma, Burke, and Martha sat at the table eating porridge. "Oh, there you are, Robby. Did you decide not to go to work so early after all?" Ma asked.

He smiled. "Got too hungry," he said, and he went to the stove to fill a bowl for himself. He told himself he would go back to City Hall as soon as Burke had left the house, but then Da came out of his bedchamber and sat at the table drinking tea. When had his father turned into a sick old man? Da's shoulders stooped. His big head lolled from one side to the other as if he didn't have the strength to hold it straight.

Robby remembered the gallows. Could he really go to the police about his father, knowing Da would be hanged? Maybe he could wait. Maybe something would happen to stop the men, something for which Robby would not be responsible.

It was a question from William Burke that sent him into action. They were at the evening meal. Da had not been drinking all day, and he appeared for supper. Mr. Burke had just passed the fried potatoes to Robby. "Martha," he said, "do you remember telling me about a poor unfortunate young woman who sleeps in the cemetery? I believe you called her Daft Jane?"

Robby stopped with his fork halfway to his lips. Were Burke and Da going after Jane? She certainly had no one who would miss her. Robby, his heart pounding, caught Martha's eye, and she understood. "I do remember, Papa, but I don't know if I told you that Jane has left Philadelphia."

"Evidently, she did not stay away long," Burke said. "I saw her just earlier today, heard her called by that name."

A hope came to Robby's mind. "Yes, I guess every person in Philadelphia could recognize Jane. She comes to the medical school often for handouts. All the students and doctors know Jane."

William Burke said nothing, but Robby could feel those evil dark eyes cutting through him, and he could eat nothing more. "I forgot, I've promised Dr. Bell I'd come back after supper. He needs me to help."

"But you've hardly touched a bite of food," said Ma.

"Likely I'll eat at the school." Robby stood, and, resisting the urge to run, walked quickly through the swinging kitchen door and out the front of the house. Once outside, he let himself break into a run. He'd check the cemetery first, and if Jane wasn't there, he would walk down every street in Philadelphia if he had to.

He did not find her among the headstones, but when he moved the branches of the willow tree he did see her blanket. She had not settled for the night. Where would she likely be? He had to make sure he found her before Burke and Da did. What would he do with her after he found her? He couldn't keep her safe for long, but he wouldn't think about that now.

The best places to look, he decided, were alleys with back doors of taverns and inns, places were she might beg for food. He began to run again. Alley after alley he saw no one but a man who had consumed too much liquor being sick to his stomach.

Finally he saw a woman who, from a distance in the darkness, looked like Jane, but when he ran to her, he could see that she was much older. She was a beggar woman, though. "Do you know Daft Jane?" he asked her.

The woman nodded her head. She muttered something, but Robby could not hear her. "I'm sorry." He leaned close. "What did you say?"

"She was here, not long ago. Got her a nice bit of food when the kitchen girl come out. She was leaving when I come, and she told me the girl might feed me next."

"Do you know where she went?"

"The cemetery, likely. She sleeps in that willow tree, lots

of room, but don't go thinking you'll get in. She screams if anyone else tries to slide inside."

Robby wished he had something to give the woman, but all he could do was call out "Thank you" as he ran. Maybe what he had said about everyone knowing Jane had made Burke change his mind, but he couldn't count on that to be true. He was out of the alley now and running hard. When he rounded the corner of a building, a lady in a shiny dress and a gentleman in a big top hat were directly in front of him. He swerved, but still he brushed against the man. "Excuse me," he shouted, but he did not slow down.

"Little ruffian," yelled the man. "I ought to catch you and teach you some manners."

A block from the graveyard, he collapsed on the steps of a huge stone house, hoping no one would come out to drive him away before he could get his breath. The moon was big and golden, lighting the street and buildings. Robby had no time to appreciate it, and he was up as soon as his breath came back to him. At last, he saw the great iron gate. It was open. He had closed it behind him. Would Jane have left it open?

He ran for the entrance, but stopped suddenly. Jane's willow tree was just inside. He had to think. Could he get her back to the Quakers and explain that her life was in danger? He wished Martha had come with him. Martha had a way with Jane, but there was no time to go for her.

Then he heard them, and he pressed himself against the wall, hoping to hide in the shadows. "Come on home with us, me girl," Da said. "Me good wife will be glad to feed you. You know me wife, and she's made a lovely meat pie."

"No," Jane's voice came from farther away. Probably she

was still beneath the willow's branches, and the men were trying to talk her into coming along peacefully. "I'm not hungry. I had a meal already, and I want to sleep."

"I'll help you sleep, all right." Burke's voice did not try to hide his impatience. "Move over, Hare," he growled. "I'll yank her out."

"Let go of my leg!" Jane screeched. "I won't go with you. I won't!"

"Stop your kicking, you wretched creature," Burke said. "Ah, I have you now."

"Let me go!" Jane's scream split the air.

"Move, Hare, get that gag in her."

Jane got out one more scream, and then she was quiet. Robby moved quickly to the corner. He could hide there and see them take her out, but what next? What was he going to do to stop them? He saw them then. They dragged Jane between them, each man holding an arm. He could not see a gag. They must have stuffed her mouth full of something. There was only one thing to do.

He stepped from the darkness. "Let her go," he said, and he felt pleased that his voice sounded strong to his own ears.

"It's your brat," said Burke. "Tell him to get lost."

"Go on home, Robby," Da said. "We don't need you here."

"But Jane does." He backed away from the men. "Let her go now."

Burke laughed. "And why, pray tell, should we listen to a snot-nosed child such as you? Get away from us at once, or you shall be most heartily sorry."

"If you don't let her go right now, I am going to the police." He was running then, running hard among the graves. Too late, he realized he had not gone toward the gate. He heard quick steps behind him, but he only looked back once. Da and Burke, holding a rope, were both running after him. Jane was nowhere to be seen. He hoped she had enough wits about her to know that she should not go back to the willow tree.

Robby risked another look over his shoulder. Da had stopped running and was bent over, holding his sides. Burke seemed to be slowing too, but he continued to move. Robby was on the other side of the cemetery now. He looked at the stone wall. If he could climb over, Burke might go running by, but he would have to be quick. There were some stones with edges that jutted out enough to allow him to grasp them, then to climb up, putting his feet where his hands had been. He was almost at the top when he slipped and landed on his back.

There was no time to try again. He spotted a big monument and just had time to hide behind it. He heard Burke moving about nearby. "Come back here, you little fool. I only want to talk to you," he called.

"Robby!" His father's voice sounded even closer than Burke's had. For an instant he thought how he had resented his father for not using his name. Now that name was being used to call him to his death.

Would Da actually allow Burke to kill him? Probably he would, to save his own neck. Besides, he wasn't sure Da could prevent Burke from committing the murders even if he wanted to. Which way should he run? What if he ran right into one of the men?

Trying to make himself as flat as possible, he pressed against the stone. Then suddenly Da was there, only a couple of feet away and staring right at Robby. For a moment they looked into each other's eyes, neither of them speaking. Every muscle in Robby's body tightened. For a second, Da put his finger to his lips in a silence gesture, and then he turned and moved away. "He ain't over here, Burke," Da called. Da had lied to his partner, lied to protect Robby. The thought amazed him, but he had no time to think more.

Burke yelled again. "He's bound to be in here. Find him, Hare. Find him now!" The sound of the voice in the night sent a chill through Robby. "I'm coming over there to have a look for myself."

Robby knew he had to move. Leaving the monument, he stepped forward cautiously. Then he tripped and fell, landing hard. He had fallen over a shovel, probably left behind when some grave robber had been disturbed at his work. Maybe he could use the shovel as a weapon. He picked it up and put it over his shoulder.

When he looked down, he froze for a second, realizing he stood at the head of Ruth's grave. He began to dig furiously, careful to throw the dirt only on the other end of the grave, not beside it. When he hit the coffin, he leaned down and jerked hard. The part of the lid Da had broken moved. One more yank, and it was up. First he put in the shovel. Then he climbed in, and pulled the lid piece back into place, careful to leave a crack for air.

Anyone looking closely at the grave would see that it had been disturbed, but his pursuers would be moving quickly and in the dark. It felt strange to be in a coffin almost covered with dirt. He heard the steps of a running man, not heavy enough to be Da, and he felt almost too scared to breathe.

Then he heard his father's voice. "We got to give it up," he called. "The boy's climbed over the wall. He must have."

Burke's voice came to him, but he could not make out the words. Now what? How long would they wait before leaving the cemetery? When he finally climbed from this grave, would he be able to get to a policeman before Burke found him? And what about Jane? Did they have her already?

It seemed colder in the coffin, mostly beneath the earth, cold and darker than he had ever experienced. His mind went back to Ruth and to how he and Da had pulled her body from the grave. She had been wrapped, he remembered, in a soft white blanket. Robby pictured how he had uncovered her face to put the rope around her. Was he lying on the blanket now? He must be. If he moved enough to get it over him, maybe he would not be so cold.

Sure enough, he found the edge of the soft fabric. He rolled to his side and lifted the top part of his body and the same time he jerked. Good! The top part of the blanket was free. He doubled his knees and lifted them, but he couldn't reach far enough to get a good hold on the blanket. He lay back down with part of the blanket under him and part covering his shoulders and stomach. Ruth's dress lay near his head, and he tried to throw it over his legs. Suddenly he wondered what had killed Ruth. Surely he had heard someone at the funeral say, but he couldn't remember such a remark. Maybe she had some terrible disease, and maybe he would catch it by lying where she had lain. He began to shiver.

Just then he heard their voices again. At first he could not make out the words, but as they got closer, he heard Burke saying, "Well, Hare, your boy has royally ruined this evening's commerce. God only knows what became of the wretched woman, and your worthless son may even as we speak be telling the police about our little business."

"I don't believe Robby would do that, not really. He'd not want to see me swing."

Burke laughed. "You think not? I find that interesting, since you've been pursuing him for some time now with the aim of doing him in."

Da answered, but Robby could not catch the words. They must have walked away, because for a moment, no sound came to him. Then suddenly a shout split the quiet. "Stop, in the name of the law." Could it be true? Was a policeman in the cemetery?

"Put up your hands." Another voice, this one with a heavy Irish accent. "You're under arrest." More than one policeman must be here. Robby pushed open the casket and, with the blanket still about him, he stood.

"Saints preserve us!" shouted the policeman with the accent. "A spirit comes up from the grave."

"No!" Robby dropped the blanket and scrabbled onto the level ground. "I was hiding from those men." He pointed toward Da and Burke, who stood some twenty feet away, their hands in the air.

"Robby!" Martha came running toward him from behind one of the three policemen. "Are you all right?" She wore a white jacket, and in the moonlight her fair hair looked white too. He thought she looked like an angel, and he knew it had been Martha who had gone to the police to save his life.

"Martha, my darling," said Burke. There was great anguish in his voice, and Robby found himself actually feeling sorry for the man. "Oh, dear, dear child!" His voice shook with emotion. "I never wanted you to know about this unpleasant business. I am so dreadfully sorry."

Martha did not go to him. "Papa," she said, "you are sorry I learned about your murders, not sorry for killing people."

"Off with you," a policeman said. "We got a little ride to take you on."

Burke and Da began to move toward the gate, two policemen behind them. One officer turned back. "Will you two young ones be all right now? You've got a place to go?"

"Yes," said Robby. "We will be fine." He stood with Martha, watching their fathers, arms over their heads, being marched out of the cemetery. "Thank you for saving my life," he said.

She nodded. "I think we should go home now. Your mother will be frantic. She told me how to find the policemen, but she doesn't know what happened after that."

Robby sighed. "Well, I am glad to hear she wouldn't just stand by and let Da kill me." He laughed a nervous little laugh. "I wasn't sure, not at all. Oh," he said, "how did you know where to find me?"

"Jane told us. She came and told us the whole story about how you saved her. You know, I think she may not be as daft as people think. She remembered her warning to you too, you know, about people watching you. She talked about feeling you were in danger. It's strange." She shook her head. "Anyway, she was scared enough to go back to the Quakers, or at least she said she would."

When they were near enough to see the Hare home, they also saw Ma walking up and down in front. "Robby, God be praised, you are alive!" Ma cried. Robby leaned his head against her for a moment. "And your da? Where is he?"

"Martha brought the policemen and they took Da away. Mr. Burke too."

Ma stepped back and buried her face in her hands. "What will become of us? What will become of us all?"

"Right now," said Robby, "we will go inside to our rest." That night he slept well for the first time in many days.

CHAPTER ELEVEN

Life in the house with the broken stoop went on. The next morning, even before breakfast, Robby went to the shed to get the ROOMS TO LET sign. There it was, behind the wheelbarrow. He wished he knew where his father had stolen the cart. He would have liked to return it. When the sign was hammered into the ground, he went in to help his mother. Robby had imagined how nice it would be to be free of the dread that had hung over them for so long, and he was glad to have had a night of sleep without the fear of murder being committed in his own home. Still, times were hard.

Early that same day three policemen came to their door. They went into each downstairs room, and then all three went upstairs to poke about. Robby, his mother, and Martha stood in the parlor listening to the footsteps, the opening and closing of doors, and the sliding of furniture. The older of the three had seemed to be in charge, and he came back down to the parlor. He took a small pencil and pad from his jacket pocket. "Take a seat," he said.

The three of them crowded onto the settee, Martha

between Robby and his mother. Robby could feel Martha's body shaking, and he saw fear in his mother's eyes. Were they all about to be arrested? The policeman settled in the brown chair. "Like I told you, I'm Sergeant Wilson," he said, "and I'd like to ask you some questions." He cleared his throat and leaned toward them. "Why did you not go to the authorities when you first learned about the murders?"

Ma looked at Robby, and he knew she wanted him to answer. "We were afraid, sir," Robby said. "William Burke would have just as soon killed us as any of the people he brought off the street." Martha gave a little gasp, and Robby added, "Well, not Martha. Her father loves Martha, but not the rest of us. Even my father feared for his life."

Sergeant Wilson wrote on his pad for a moment. "How many?" he asked. "The number of murders, I mean."

Robby and his mother exchanged looks. Robby bit at his lower lip. "Two for sure, probably three," he said. "The two were a man and a woman. We don't know their names. I don't think there was any connection between them." The sergeant wrote on his pad.

"We tried not to notice, not to think about what went on upstairs." Ma's voice shook. "We done what we had to do, don't you know, so to survive."

"To survive," Sergeant Wilson repeated, and again he wrote on his pad. "One more question," he said. "What day did Burke first rent the rooms?"

"It was early spring, April I think," said Robby. He heard Martha make a little swallowing sound, and then to his surprise she spoke.

"April third, that's the day we came to Philadelphia on the

train, just two days after my mama died." Martha grasped Robby's hand and Ma's. She leaned forward. "Sergeant," she said, "we used to live in Boston. My papa might have killed my uncle there."

The two other policemen had come downstairs during the last question, and all three of them went to the door. "Don't leave Philadelphia," the sergeant said just before he stepped out the door. "Not until after the trials. You'll be required to serve as witnesses, and you have to be there. It's the law."

And so they lived in dread of the trial, but the need for money was quickly a bigger problem. The money from Miss Stone's rent was almost gone. They needed food and money for coal to be able to cook their meals. Robby collected his pay from Dr. Bell, and that helped. They packed up Burke's belongings, and Robby planned to sell them and Miss Stone's trunk to a man on Second Street who bought such items. He would use the wheelbarrow to carry the things over.

They hoped each day that someone would come to take a room, but for days the sign brought no one. Finally, an elderly woman in a big hat came to inquire. Robby opened the door when she knocked, and he invited her into the hall. His mother came then and introduced herself. The woman began to shake her head. "Oh, dear, no, I didn't know this was the house. I couldn't live where those bloody murders took place. Dear me, no." Still shaking her head, she backed out the front door.

"We may have to sell this house, if we can. I'm afraid no one will rent a room from us, not until after this terrible business dies down," Ma said as she sank down on the third stair. "I'm going to the jail," she said. "I'll go this very day and ask to see your da."

Martha had come halfway down, and she asked, "May I go with you? I'd like to see Papa."

"Yes, child, we may not be allowed in, but we can ask." Ma pulled herself up by the rail. "Will you go with me, son?"

Robby's chest felt tight, as if he might not be able to breathe. "Ma," he said, "I can't. Oh, I know at the last he lied to Burke about seeing me." He shook his head. "But look at this mess we're in. I'm not ready to forgive him."

His mother reached out to brush his hair away from his face. "He loves you, Robby. I don't believe he would have let anything happen to you."

"He wouldn't have killed me, maybe, but I think he would have stood by and let his partner do it. You say today that you don't believe it, but that awful night there was danger enough for you to send Martha for the police." He looked back at her.

Ma sighed, and wiped her hand across her face. "He's still your da, Robby." She looked up at Martha. "We'll go right now, else I might lose my nerve."

Robby followed his mother into the kitchen, where she took bread and cheese, wrapped it in a cloth, and put it in a small basket. "It's a good long walk to Walnut Street. That's where the jail is. We'll be wanting something for our noon meal before we get back."

Robby stood at the front window, watching Martha and his mother walk away. Just before they rounded the first corner, he ran after them. "I'll just walk along with you, but I won't go in."

It was the first week of June, and the weather was beautiful. The mountain laurel shrubs about the city were in full pink and white bloom. Robby could almost believe that the little group had set out for a pleasure walk. On one street, they passed a small house with a fence around it. A boy held a pan and fed a goat from it. "Look, Martha," Robby said, "there's Lucy and her boy." For just an instant a light of amusement came to Martha's eyes, but it did not last long.

"Yonder's the jail," Ma said when they could see the big stone building. "God help us. I never thought I'd be here to see a murderer."

His mother did not pressure Robby more to go inside. "Here," she said, and she handed him the basket. "Don't eat it all afore we get back." He watched them climb the front steps. A tree grew on some grass in front of the building, and he settled himself on the ground to watch the people and to wonder what business each of them had in the jail.

A woman came up the sidewalk and sent two small children to sit near him. The little boy and girl kept their eyes on Robby. "What are your names?" he asked, but they did not answer. Their staring made him uncomfortable, and he felt glad when their mother returned. The children ran to her, chattering in a foreign language. As they walked away, the girl looked over her shoulder and waved at Robby.

Martha came out before Ma. Robby could see she had been crying. She wiped at her eyes and tried to smile when she saw him. "I know you hate him. I understand that, but I don't hate him, just what he did."

He nodded. "I don't hate my da either," he told her. "I wish I could, but I don't."

"Papa wants me to write to my aunt Susan, and he told me where he has money hidden in the cane. He told me to buy a train ticket to Boston. I am to take half of what is left, and give you the rest."

"What? He wants you to give me money? The man wanted to kill me!"

Martha shrugged her shoulders. "He isn't all bad, Robby. I can't explain my papa, not in a hundred years, but he isn't all bad."

"When will you go to Boston?" Robby was surprised by the lump in his throat when he thought of Martha's leaving.

"After the trial. I'll have to stay until then. I didn't tell Papa that the policeman said we would have to testify. It would only fret him about me being there and having to answer questions."

Robby saw his mother coming down the steps. "Here comes Ma," he said. "Don't mention the money to her. I'll tell you why later."

When she reached them, she said nothing at first, only took the basket from Robby and handed out the bread and cheese. They ate as they walked. "He told me he would not have let Burke hurt you." She stopped walking and reached out to stop Robby by taking his arm. "He wanted you to know that he wouldn't ever have let Burke kill you."

Robby pulled his arm free and began to walk again. "That's not how it seemed to me, Ma, not while I was shivering and shaking down in that coffin. It sure did not feel to me like Da was on my side."

When they were home, Martha brought down her father's cane. "I'm glad you didn't sell this before we found out about the money." She handed the cane to Robby. "Papa said unscrew the top, but I couldn't budge it."

Robby grasped the golden top and leaned, putting all his weight into it. The top gave slightly. He tried again, and this time it came off in his hand. Slipping his finger into the hollow stick, he pulled out several bills. They fell to the floor, and Martha gathered them into her hand, counting.

"There's one hundred and fifty dollars here," she said, and she handed all the bills to Robby. "You and your mother take it all for now. You can give me back enough for a train ticket when we find out how much the fare is."

Robby picked out one of the bills. "I'm only going to give Ma this for now. Twenty dollars will do her for a month or so. Maybe by then we will know more about what will happen to Da. If he should get out somehow, he'd make her give him whatever she had." He looked about the parlor. There were Miss Stone's books. "I'll put the rest of this in *Doctor Bodkin's Complete Guide to Home Treatment of the Human Body*." He went to the big book, opened it, and slipped the bills inside. "This way, you will know where it is if you need it."

"I don't know where that money came from. It's bound to be from the bodies or from cheating at cards." Her face looked distressed. "Do you think we should give it to Sergeant Wilson?"

"I suspect we should," he said, "but the police wouldn't know where it came from either. We just won't worry about where your papa got it. We need it too much."

The next day Robby went back to work again at the medical college. He had been there only once since his father's arrest. He had dreaded that first time that there would be questions from Dr. Bell or from Lij, but neither of them had mentioned his father or his crimes. Still, this time, when Dr. Bell called out to him as he walked by the open door to his office, he did not want to go inside, leaning instead on the door frame, ready to make a quick getaway. "We have another cadaver in room five," Dr. Bell said.

"What's a cadaver?"

"It is a term used by doctors for the bodies we dissect for research and for education." The doctor smiled at him. "You know, Robby, you would be welcome anytime to go up in the observation stand and watch." The doctor leaned across his desk, and his voice was quieter. "It might actually help you. Oh, not to make murder right, of course not." He shook his head. "Still, it might help you some to see how much our students learn. Do you know some doctors are so eager to learn that they dissect members of their own family? After they die, of course."

Robby stepped away from the door. "I might," he said, and he nodded. "Yes, I just might." He walked away then, but he noticed when the students began to gather in room five, and he slipped inside and climbed the stairs.

Dr. Bell was holding up something that Robby recognized from the charts to be a heart. "There are four chambers inside this organ," the doctor said. Robby leaned forward, fascinated. For a long time, he watched Dr. Bell and listened to his explanation. When he knew the group was about to be dismissed, he went down and out the door.

Neither Martha nor Ma returned to the jail. The papers were full of stories about Burke and Hare, and it was from a newspaper that Robby learned his father's fate. "Get your paper here," a newsboy called from the corner one day as Robby was about to cross the street. "Hare gives evidence against Burke." Robby had a coin in his pocket, and he held it out the boy.

"Give me a paper," he said.

"Sure thing," said the boy. "You want to read about Burke and Hare, huh?"

"Yes," said Robby. "They are an interesting pair."

He took the paper and walked to the cemetery. There he sat on a bench and read the story. Roger Hare, the paper said, had given evidence against William Burke, claiming that Burke was the one who actually killed the people. Boston police had sent telegrams about Burke's theft and the murder of his brother-in-law. In exchange for his testimony, Hare was promised an early release from jail. Robby read that his father would be free in September under the condition that he leave Philadelphia, never to return. Burke would go to trial sometime in August. Robby did not tell his mother or Martha about what he had learned. He would, he told himself, tell when the time was right, but somehow the right time did not seem to come.

Then one day on the same street corner, he bought another paper. This one had headlines that read BURKE GOES TO TRIAL. Robby stood still, reading. Burke, he learned, would go to trial in five days. Now Robby knew he had to talk about what he had read. He waited until after supper. He told them at the table while they drank tea. "Your papa is to go to trial in five days," he said to Martha, and he took the newspaper from beside him on the chair and laid it on the table.

"I want to go upstairs to read this," Martha said, and she slipped from her chair.

When Martha was gone, Robby turned to his mother. "Da will be free in September because he has agreed to testify against Burke. He had to promise, though, to leave Philadelphia and to never return."

"Leave Philadelphia?" Ma shook her head. "Where will we go?" She looked about the kitchen. "How will we live without this place to rent?"

"Ma." Robby reached out to put his hand on his mother's arm. "You can't go with him. You and I can run this place just like we've always done, or better yet, we can sell this house and buy another one. I've been thinking we ought to change our names too."

His mother pushed her chair back from the table. "Your mind's made up. You won't go with us, will you, Robby?"

"No. I am finished with living in fear of Da, and you should be too."

"I don't know, Robby. I just don't know."

He too pushed away from the table. "You will have to know soon," he said, and he left the room.

The next day a man brought a legal notice to the door. Robby, his mother, and Martha were all required to be at the courthouse on August 14, the first day of the trial. They would be compelled to testify against William Burke. With the notice in his hand, Robby wandered into the kitchen, where his mother bent over the big laundry tub. He sat down at the table and read the notice aloud to her. "Poor little girl, she'll take this fearsome hard," Ma said.

"She will. It's three days yet before we have to go. Maybe we shouldn't tell her until then."

Ma dried her hands and arms on her apron. "No, I'd not feel right keeping it from her. Might as well go up and get it over with."

Robby followed her upstairs. Martha's door was open. She sat at her table writing, the kitten curled at her feet. Alarmed by their faces, she stood up as they came in. "What's wrong?" she said. "There's bad news, isn't there?"

Robby handed her the paper. She read it then let the notice drop from her hand to the floor. "I can't do it," she cried, and she buried her face in her hands.

"I think you have to," said Ma. "It's the law, child."

On the morning of August 14, they had to leave early for the walk to the courthouse on Chestnut Street. Robby knew the sun was hot, and he started to protest when Martha came down the stairs wearing her heavy cape. He decided to let his mother handle the situation.

"Wait here," he said. "I'll tell Ma we are ready."

When he returned, his mother followed him. "Oh no," Ma said. "You'll pass out from heat dressed that way." She reached out to remove the cape.

Martha looked at the floor. "I wanted something to cover me," she murmured.

Hannah handed her the cape. "Take this back upstairs. I'll get something for you to wear." Robby's knees felt shaky, and he sat on the stairway to wait.

His mother came back with a black lace shawl, and Robby remembered that Da had come home with it the night that Lolly died. "Here." Ma held out the shawl. "This will make you feel better."

The walk seemed shorter than when they had first gone to the jail. On one corner, Robby noticed a small blond girl. She held out matches as people passed. He waited until they were directly across the street so that he could be sure, then said, "Look, Martha, it's Dolly, the little match girl."

"Oh," said Martha. "I am so glad to see her. She looks well. Remember how Papa gave me money for her? You do remember that, don't you?"

"I do," he said. He'd have to remember to pay her a visit once all this was over. Too soon the cupolas on top of the courthouse could be seen in the distance. When they were closer, they saw a crowd standing about the building and on the steps. They stopped for a moment to rest. "We'd better go in," said Ma, "before they come out looking for us." She took Martha's arm, and Robby shoved open a path for them through the crowd.

The courtroom was already packed. Robby could see William Burke sitting with another man at a table toward the front. A wooden rail separated them from the general seating. Another table stood on the left; a gentleman in a waistcoat sat at it, his suit jacket hanging from the back of his chair. In the middle were twelve empty chairs, and Robby knew they must be for the jury. The judge's bench was empty, and so was the boxlike area where he supposed the witnesses would have to stand.

They found three places on the left, toward the back of the room. Martha had the shawl pulled up over her head and shoulders, and she gripped the edges tightly with both hands. Ma sat between Robby and Martha. Shortly after they were settled in their places, the twelve men of the jury filed in from a door to the left. Next, a voice called out, "All rise," and everyone stood up.

"The judge is coming in," Ma whispered.

"Do you see Da?" Robby whispered back, and his mother shook her head. Robby was glad his father was not in the room. Maybe he could say his piece or get his questions answered or whatever it was he had to do before they brought in his da. Robby did not want to see the man, not ever again.

When he sat back down, Robby folded his arms front of himself and deliberately tried to block out the voices of the men at the front of the room. He did hear the state's lawyer say that Burke was guilty of four murders. Next he heard the words he had dreaded. "The prosecution calls its first witness, Miss Martha Burke."

"No!" The scream filled the room. "No, not my little daughter!" Burke was on his feet now, and Robby could see the chains that fastened him to the huge wooden table. "Leave my daughter alone. I confess," Burke yelled. "I am guilty as charged."

The crowd went wild, everyone talking at once. Ma put her arm around Martha, who leaned against her and sobbed. "There, there," Ma whispered. "The man's evil, no denying, but you were the goodness inside him. Hold that as your comfort, child. He loves you more than he loves his wicked self."

Robby looked around the room. Lots of people were standing up, many of them talking to people in front of or behind them. There were men, women, and a few children. The only familiar face he saw was that of Father Francis, who sat near the back on the other side of the room. His eyes were closed, and Robby wondered if he was praying. "Order in the court. Order in the court," shouted the judge, and he banged his wooden hammer hard against his huge desk. "Order, or I'll have the room cleared."

People sat back down and stopped talking. "Mr. Quinn," the judge continued, "would you please approach the bench?" The gentleman who had sat with William Burke went forward to speak privately with the judge. Then a man in uniform used a big key to unlock the chain that held Burke to the table. His hands and feet were chained, but he could walk slowly and was led up to the judge.

The room was totally quiet, and Robby could see that most people leaned forward, as if hoping to catch a snatch of the conversation that went on among the judge, Burke, and his attorney. Finally, the judge nodded. Burke was led hobbling back to his place, but neither he nor his lawyer sat down.

"William Burke," the judge said clearly. "In light of your full confession, there will be no more discussion." He paused and looked about the room. "It is now my duty to pass sentence upon you. I hereby sentence you to be hanged by the neck until dead. The sentence will be carried out two weeks and two days from now, on the first day of September. This court is dismissed."

CHAPTER TWELVE

The next day, Martha left Philadelphia. Robby and his mother walked with her to the train station. Robby carried her suitcase, and his mother carried a large hatbox that had belonged to Miss Stone. Several holes had been punched through the box lid. Martha held her cat, Alley, who would be put into the box before Martha got on the train.

No one talked during the walk. Tears occasionally ran down Martha's cheek, but she would hold Alley in one hand and wipe her face with the other. Robby feared his mother was going to cry at any minute, but Ma did not cry easily. He had not seen her cry during the last horrible weeks. Robby was afraid if she started to cry now, she would not be able to stop. He was also afraid he would join her.

When they got to the station, Robby was surprised to see only three cars behind the engine. A man in a uniform stood on the ground taking tickets from people, who then climbed the steps and went through the open door of the second car. "I'll write to you," Robby said when they stopped beside the car.

Martha nodded, swallowing back tears. "Will you put Alley in the box?" she asked.

He took the cat. Ma held the box top while Martha held the box. "She's a deal bigger than when we got her from that tree," Robby said, and he set Alley in the box.

"Oh, Robby . . ." Martha could say no more for sobbing. Ma gathered Martha, box and all, to her for a hug.

"I'll write to you," Robby said again, because he could think of nothing else to say, and he gave Martha a quick kiss on the cheek.

"All aboard!" the railway man called. Robby handed him Martha's ticket and bag, and she climbed the steps.

Robby and Ma looked for her in the train windows, but the window seats were all full of other people. Still, they waited until the engine pulled the cars away.

"Poor little mite," Ma said. "I pray she finds a bit of joy in Boston. She's had enough weeping for a lifetime." She moved to a bench. "I've need of a wee rest." She sank onto the seat, almost melting into the wood. Robby wondered if she would ever be able to get up. He wandered a few feet away and stood watching the train until the last sight of it disappeared over the horizon. He stayed in the spot, looking in that direction for a long time.

Finally, he turned back to his mother on the bench. He held out his hand to help her. "Come on, Ma," he said. "We may as well head home."

"I'd have liked to have kept her," Ma said when they had started to walk. "I'd truly have liked to have kept her, but your da . . ."

"Please don't talk to me about Da," said Robby, and he began to walk faster, leaving his mother behind.

Later that same day, he discovered that Martha had taken only enough of the money to buy her train ticket. There were still several bills left in the big book. William Burke's money was all his now, to do with as he chose. He stared down at the bills and imagined Burke's white hands counting them, rolling them, and sliding them into the hollow cane. The picture made him shudder, and he jammed the money into his pocket.

He walked into the kitchen and called to his mother, who was lying down in her bedchamber, "I'm going to the school." Poor worn thing; his heart softened toward her, and he went into the room. She lay with her eyes closed, but he was certain she was not asleep. "I'll be back for supper with you, Ma. I'll bring home food from a street vendor."

"You're a good boy, you are," she said without opening her eyes.

On the street, Robby turned toward St. Mary's. No Mass was being said in the middle of the afternoon, and Robby was relieved to see no one about the church grounds. He slipped into the dark building, where the smell of burning candles filled the air. He stood near the door until his eyes adjusted to the lack of light. Father Francis was nowhere to be seen. Robby went to the big metal collection box fastened to a great wooden table. The box was locked, but a small slit in the top allowed money to be deposited. Robby had seen his mother drop an occasional coin in the box, but the Hare family had never put in bills. "This is from my da, Roger Hare, and from Mr. William Burke," he said aloud, and one after the other he pushed the bills through the slot. He went quickly to the altar, genuflected, then hurried from the building.

At the hospital, he worked for a couple of hours, then asked Dr. Bell for his wages. "If it's all right, I'd like to come to work every day now for a couple of hours," Robby said after he had asked for his money. He had gone with the doctor into room five, where Dr. Bell took the three dollars from the metal box he kept for resurrection men.

"Certainly. I've noticed that Lij gets slower and slower." He handed Robby the money and returned the box to the shelf. "I am sure he will be glad to let you take over more of his work. Are you and your mother in need of money, Robby?"

Robby shook his head. "We can do with what I make if I work two hours every day, and I've got quite a lot of things to sell. Thank you, doctor," he said, and he left the room.

On the street he bought some oysters and some cooked ears of corn to take home to Ma for supper. Robby knew he could take care of himself and his mother. He tried not to think about his father's release.

He was reading in the parlor that evening when a knock sounded on the front door. Just enough daylight was left for him to see through the window that Father Francis stood on the stoop. Father Francis had only been at the Hare home once before, when Lolly died. Then Robby thought of the money. The priest must have come about the money he had put into the box. Had he seen Robby? Maybe he had even heard what Robby said, and maybe he had come to say the church did not want such dirty money. He swallowed hard before he opened the door and said, "Come in, Father."

Ma had heard the knock from the kitchen and came

through the swinging door. "Father Francis," she said, "we are pleased to have you call. Take a seat, won't you?" Her voice was nervous, and she turned to Robby. "Get Father a cup of tea. The water's still hot."

Robby moved quickly across the room and was about to go into the kitchen when the priest held up his hand. "No, no tea for me, please." He sat down in the chair. "I'll not tarry long, but I've just come from the jail. I saw Roger, and he asked me to tell you to meet him on Wednesday at ten. He's being released."

Ma lowered her body onto the settee. "Day after tomorrow," she whispered. "They're letting him go on the day they hang Burke. Did you know that, Father? I mean about the hanging being on Wednesday."

"Yes, Hannah, I knew. I'll give last rites to William Burke just before . . ." He looked about the room. "His little girl, Martha, I believe that's her name, is she here?"

"Gone to Boston on the train this very morning." Ma looked down at her apron and smoothed it across her middle.

"Good, I'll tell Mr. Burke. That's what he wanted, her gone from the city before the execution." The priest cleared his throat. "Roger told me he must leave Philadelphia." He leaned to look into Ma's face.

" 'Tis so." Ma did not look up.

"Will the two of you be going as well?"

"I can't say, not as yet."

Robby had remained near the kitchen door, and he spoke from there. "I can say. I won't be going."

Father Francis nodded. "I'll pray for the both of you, and, of course, for Roger. He's mightily sorry for his sins."

"Da's been sorry before," said Robby, and he went through the swinging door.

"I'll pray for you, Robby, pray that God takes away your anger," the priest called, and then Robby heard him say that he must go. He also heard Ma follow him and express her gratitude for the visit and the prayers.

Robby went to the cabinet, took his pallet, and spread it on the floor. It occurred to him then that he could sleep upstairs. He had no desire to go into the room where the bodies had been kept or into William Burke's room, but he could sleep in Martha's. Maybe he would do that tomorrow night. He would also open the windows in the other two rooms, and the doors too. He would leave them that way for days, letting all the bad air blow out of the place. He pretended to be asleep when his mother passed through the kitchen on her way to bed.

The next day Robby made four trips with the wheelbarrow to Bran's. He had passed the shop many times, and had seen the sign that read BRAN'S DRY GOODS AND SUNDRIES. In smaller letters were the words WE BUY AND SELL. It was a large store with little light. Robby had lined the cart with newspaper and had stacked Miss Stone's clothes, shoes, brushes, gloves, and the pretty cups and saucers she liked to use for tea inside.

"Three dollars," the tall thin man who ran the shop said when Robby had shown him all the goods.

Robby took the bills, thanked the man, and told him he would be back.

A small lady with flowers in her hat followed him from the store. "Boy," she called with an Italian accent, "you should get more." She moved her thumb across the tips of her fingers.

"You know, more money. You give them too cheap. Got to . . ." She hesitated, searching for the word. "You got to bargain." She nodded. "Yes, you got to bargain."

"Thank you," said Robby, and when he brought back Miss Stone's trunk, he shook his head at the first offer. "Oh, no," he said, "I'd rather keep it than let it go for that." He left with six more dollars. He was able to get eight dollars for all of Burke's fancy clothes and tall hat.

"You rob me, lad," Bran grumbled when he handed over ten dollars for the cane with the secret hiding place.

Robby laughed. "Runs in the family, I guess." At home he hurried through the house to find his mother in the kitchen rocker, her mending on her lap. "I got nineteen dollars altogether, Ma." He waved the bills at her. "We can live a month on this, maybe more," he said. "By that time, we can likely rent a room or two."

She stood up and moved toward the window, leaving her work on the chair and turning her back on her son. Robby's gaze fell on the rocker and Da's shirt. "You're working on this?" He picked up the shirt and held it out away from his body.

"He has to have something on his back, Robby. You know he does."

"Go ahead, Ma, tell me. You're going with him, aren't you?"

She turned back to face him. "He needs me, son. You come too, please, Robby." She reached out to take hold of his arm. "He's your da. We can start over someplace. Father Francis will sell this house for us. I asked him today."

Robby pulled away from her. He counted out ten dollars and threw the money on the table. "Here, Ma, here's your share of the money. I won't be coming with you, and I won't be coming home tonight. Good-bye, Ma." He ran through the back door and down the alley. For a long time he walked around the city. He moved through the streets, knowing he would go eventually to the medical school. Lij would take him in at least for the night, but he did not want to go until bedtime. If it was time for sleep, Lij would not ask as many questions.

Robby bought roasted chestnuts from a street vendor and ate them as he walked. Next he bought one tulip from a little girl who sold flowers on the corner of Adams Street. "What you going to do with this?" the little girl wanted to know.

"Take it to my little sister," he said.

At the cemetery, he laid the flower on the grave. "Ma and Da are leaving this town," he said aloud. "Leaves just you and me in Philly." He wandered out of the big iron gate. For a while he stood outside the almshouse owned by the Quakers. He sat for a time on the stone steps, wondering if he should go in and ask to see Daft Jane. He decided not to. What if Jane turned out to be miserable? He could do nothing to help her, and he could not bear seeing another sorrow.

Without thinking, he wandered into Northwest Square. There he looked up at the wooden structure being built, and his stomach lurched. He thought he might throw up the nuts he just ate. He folded his arms across his stomach, closed his eyes, and leaned for a time against a lamppost. He didn't understand why his stomach acted up so. Didn't he know better than most people that Burke deserved to be hanged? Hadn't the man ruined life in the house with the broken stoop?

Finally, just after darkness settled on the city, he knocked at the wooden door of the medical school. "I need a place to sleep," he told Lij when the man opened the door.

"Sure thing." Lij led Robby down the hall to the open door of his small room. Inside, Lij handed him a blanket. "Unfold that cot." He pointed to a folded bed leaning against the wall. "I brung it in a while ago. Figured you would need it."

Robby did as he was told, and Lij blew out the candle. Robby was relieved that Lij had asked no questions, but in the dark, he said, "I know about your father. Reckon everybody in town knows about him and Burke." Robby said nothing, and Lij added, "You eat anything, son?"

"Yes," Robby said softly.

"Doc would be glad if you stayed here. You could let in the resurrection men and give them their money. That way, Doc could go to his own bed at night. You could do that, couldn't you? Seeing the bodies brought in wouldn't be too much for you to stand?"

"No," said Robby, "that doesn't bother me now." Then the small room was quiet. For a long time, no sleep came to him. He lay awake listening to Lij snore and smelling the strong cleaning substance used in the school. Finally, after what seemed like hours and hours, sleep came and blocked out the pain.

In the morning, Lij woke him. "Get up, lad. I've got some bread for ye and a bit of sausage." For a second Robby couldn't remember where he was, but he sat up and rubbed his eyes. Lij put a saucer on the tiny table. "Got to get to work now," he said, and he shuffled out.

The food filled Robby's stomach, and gratitude to Lij and Dr. Bell filled his heart. Robby would give Lij part of his money from Dr. Bell for food. He looked about the room. Yes, he could live here.

He wandered out into the hall. The big clock said eight thirty. His mother would meet his father in an hour and a half. He looked at his hands, surprised that they were not shaking. He felt shaky inside, far too nervous to work. He would walk. Maybe he would go to the square to see how the gallows had progressed. Why should he do that? Hadn't it made him sick to see the structure the day before? Still, once outside, he found himself heading in that direction.

There it was. A rope now dangled over a trapdoor that hung open. People stood about in small groups. Robby stopped walking and sank down at the base of a tree. A family sat on the other side, a mother, a father, and two boys. He noticed a basket, covered with a cloth. Was there food in there? Had that family come to have a picnic and see Burke hang? His whole body felt shaky, and he reached out to hold the tree for help in pulling himself up. Whirling away, he almost bumped into a lady selling oysters. "I'm sorry," he muttered.

"Buy yourself some oysters, lad," she said. "You'll want to have something to eat while you watch him swing."

Robby shook his head. The woman leaned closer to him. "Don't go drifting off and lose your good view. Crowd going to be big way before ten."

"Is that when it happens, ten?"

"So they say, boy." She laughed. "Ain't it a hoot? They'll give his body to the doctors to cut up, just like the poor souls he murdered. Oysters, oysters, roasted oysters." She walked on.

Robby stood still, but his mind raced. They would hang Burke at the same time they let Da out of jail. A voice from the other side of the tree broke into his thoughts. "Which one are they hanging, Papa? Is it Burke or Hare?"

"Burke," said the man. "Hare got off by talking about Burke."

"Tell us the story again about what they done."

Robby moved away quickly. Ten o'clock would be here soon. His mother and father would be leaving the city. He knew what he had to do. He started to run, dodging people, once narrowly missing being hit by a rider on horseback.

His mother sat on the low stone wall that separated the jail from the street. She wore the black lace shawl. Two white bags, obviously stuffed with belongings, rested at her feet. A small gasp escaped from Robby. The body bag! Ma had cut the bag in two and sewed up a second bag. For a moment Robby did not move. Then Da, or at least a thin man who resembled Da, came through the door, and Ma stood.

"Wait," Robby called, and his parents turned toward him.

"God be praised!" Ma shouted. "I knew you'd come."

"You've forgiven your old da, ain't you, Robby, me boy?" Roger Hare held out his arms.

Robby stood still and folded his arms across his chest. "I don't know, Da. I don't know if I can forgive you or not." He shrugged his shoulders. "Anyway, that's not why I came." He stuck his hand into his pocket and pulled out the money from Bran. "Here," he said, "take this. I don't need it as much as you do."

"Come with us, son, please." His mother reached out to take his arm, but he stepped away from her.

"I can't, Ma. Just take the money. When you get where you're going, maybe you can find someone to write me a letter at the medical school." It was his father who reached for the money, and for a second Robby thought of pulling it back.

He didn't. What difference did it make who took the money? Ma would give it to Da anyway. She could never break free from him.

A train whistle sounded. "We got to hurry, Robby. Got to catch a train." Tears rolled down Ma's cheek.

"Good-bye," Robby said. "I'm going to work now." He turned away.

When he knew the hanging was over, he walked through the square on his way to the school. Most of the crowd was gone, but the same group of girls he had seen before jumped rope. Their words made Robby stop and stand dead still. "Through the alley and up the stair, arm and arm come Burke and Hare, Burke the butcher, Hare the thief, Doctor, Doctor, slice the beef."

When he could move, Robby found his way to the heavy wooden door. It was locked. They were cutting up someone in room five, and he knew it was Burke. He knocked hard. Lij opened the door. "Might be best if you stay away from room five," he said.

Robby stepped back. He couldn't go inside right now. "I'm going to get my clothes and my books. Can I bring my books here?"

"Sure thing," said Lij.

Robby walked slowly and stood for a long time in front of the house with the broken stoop. In April he had lived there with five other people. They were all gone away now, all except him, and even he would be leaving soon. There would be no more Robby Hare in Philadelphia.

First he went to the shed for the wheelbarrow and parked it in front of the house. He carried the books out, several at a time, and stacked them carefully in the cart. When they were all loaded, he went into the kitchen for his clothing and blankets. He opened the back door for one last look. There was the vegetable garden that would never be planted. He bolted the door and went out front to spread what he carried across the top of the books.

He pushed the wheelbarrow away, but he looked back once at the house. He wished he could have fixed the broken stoop and the skewed shutters. At the school, the heavy wooden door was unlocked now, and Robby knew the cutting was finished. He would unload the books, then take the cart and leave it somewhere on Society Hill.

He hesitated for just a moment before he went inside. It was strange how his life had come full circle since that first terrible night he had entered the building. He no longer had to fear being forced to steal bodies in the night. Instead, he would be on the receiving side of that operation. He still hated the idea that anyone would rob graves, but he understood the need to study the human anatomy. In fact, he felt certain he would soon be involved in the learning.

Lij was in the hallway, his broom in hand. "Lij," said Robby, "I'm going to change my last name. I was thinking I might use Jenkins. Would that be all right with you?"

"I'd be mighty proud," said Lij.

Robby Jenkins, his arms full of books, moved with a lighter heart down the hallway toward the room that was his new home.

AUTHOR'S NOTE

I first became interested in bodies being stolen and sold when I went to Edinburgh, Scotland, ten years ago. It was there that I learned how the growth of medical schools brought about the need for bodies to dissect for learning purposes. Also in Edinburgh, I first heard about Burke and Hare, and about the jump rope chant using their names.

In this book, I borrowed the story of Burke and Hare from Edinburgh, where two men by those names really did kill sixteen or seventeen people in the 1820s to sell their bodies. Hare really did own a boardinghouse, and he saved his own life by testifying against Burke. The word "burking" came into our language, meaning to kill a person in order to obtain a corpse. I made up Robby and Martha, and I Americanized the chant by changing the word "close" to "alley."

The stir over Burke and Hare, at least partially, caused laws to be passed in Great Britain making it a crime to take bodies and providing that all unclaimed bodies in hospitals, prisons, and workhouses be given to medical schools.

Body stealing went on longer in America. One interesting

case occurred in 1878 in Ohio. John Scott Harrison, a member of the U.S. Congress, was the son of William Henry Harrison, who was our ninth president, and father of Benjamin Harrison, our twenty-third president. When John Scott Harrison died, the family noticed that the nearby grave of a friend had been opened and robbed. The Harrisons decided to put bars across John Scott's grave to protect it from thieves. The next day, two of the young men in the family went to the medical schools to look for the friend's body. They were horrified to find their own relative's body, stolen despite their precautions.

The outrage over this case caused laws to be passed in one state after another to stop body stealing and to give unclaimed bodies to medical schools. Finally, the people of America could bury their dead without the terrible fear that robbers would steal away those precious bodies.